COFFIN for CASH

as written by
NIK MORTON

Cover image from Shutterstock. Design by dMix.

ISBN: 978-1-943035-18-2

www.beattoapulp.com

CONTENTS

Acknowledgments

Thanks to David for asking again.

Lots of love to Jennifer, my editor, wife and friend; and to Hannah, Harry, Darius, and Suri.

PREMATURE BURIAL

Head pounding as though a dozen demented black-smiths had taken a dislike to their anvils, Cash Laramie opened his eyes. He blinked. He couldn't see anything, only darkness. Complete, overwhelming darkness. His heart lurched as he realized he was blind. He raised his right hand, intent on rubbing his eyes, but his knuckles hit hard against something solid that was covered in silken material. And his broad shoulders were barely able to shift. He blinked again and licked his parched lips, tasted the metallic flavor of dried blood.

Trying again, he was able to slide his hand to his temple and felt the dried crust of a bloody wound, which might account for the persistent throbbing headache.

He steadied his breathing.

Don't panic, he told himself.

He raised a leg, but his knee too met with an obstruction after the slightest movement.

As he couldn't see, he must rely on his other senses.

Touch told him that he was confined in a dark narrow place.

His ears detected no sound: absolute silence. No birds singing, no wagons, horses or people nearby.

He sniffed the air: it was musty, a mixture of earthiness with a hint of incense. He didn't like what that knowledge suggested.

Tamping down that bleak idea, he fumbled in his vest pocket, found his box of matches. He could move both hands together over his chest, and managed to remove a match and scratched it against the friction board.

He blinked at the buttery brightness of light, welcome light. Thank God! He wasn't blind, after all. In this confined space the smell of the burnt red phosphorus was very strong.

He was lying in a coffin lined with white silk.

And although he wondered how he'd gotten into this mess, he was convinced it all began no more than a couple of days ago ...

CHAPTER ONE

BERENICE

Only this morning, as he dressed in front of the cheval glass mirror and Lenora lounged on the bed, she had commented on his six-foot tall broad shouldered physique. "You may be almost thirty, Cash, but you could pass for a half-dozen years younger."

He'd combed a hand through his dark hair, his vibrant blue eyes lancing hers in the reflection. "Thanks, but I'm happy to be older than twenty-four, you know." He rubbed the stubble on his square jaw, noting the lines around his eyes and deeply etching from his nose to his mouth. "With age comes experience. And experience saves lives."

"You can save my life any day, lover," she'd joked.

Now, he smiled fondly at the memory as he extinguished his cheroot, pocketed it and stepped into Cheyenne's federal building.

He made his way to the office of Chief U.S. Marshal Devon Penn and knocked on the door.

"Enter!" his boss barked. So he entered.

Penn's bulk sat behind his imposing desk.

Occupying one of the two Windsor armchairs was a woman—an attractive redhead.

"Glad you made it!" Penn waved him in and Cash shut the door behind him.

He removed his black Stetson as Penn stood. "Cash, let me introduce you! This is Miss Berenice Rohmer—a family friend who needs my—our—help."

"Hello, Marshal Laramie," Berenice Rohmer said as he approached. She looked at him, her golden brown eyes shining brightly, appraising. Boldly, he returned her scrutiny. She was probably in her mid-twenties, buxom, curves pressing alluringly against the green velvet jacket; a matching hat sat askew atop her long red hair that was done up and tamed by jeweled pins. Beneath the skirt, her legs were crossed; she wore black lace-up boots with a high heel. Thin pale red lips parted slightly and then finally formed into a smile.

He returned her smile, holding out his hand. "Pleased to make your acquaintance, ma'am."

Her hand was warm, the handshake firm. "Do call me Berenice."

"Take a seat, Cash," Penn said, gesturing at the second Windsor.

As he ensconced himself in the leathery upholstery, Cash asked, "What is the nature of the help you need, ma … Berenice?"

She fumbled in her reticule and withdrew a lace handkerchief, dabbed at her retroussé nose, and then glanced at Penn, eyes pleading.

4

"I'll explain, my dear," Penn said, solicitously, double chin wobbling. He steepled his pudgy fingers, and then eyed Cash. "Berenice's brother—he's some three years her senior—well, he's a financier, and he has gone missing in the region of Rock Springs and Green River."

"What business did he have in Dakota territory?" Cash wondered.

"You've heard of the new casino there?" Penn said.

"Yes, of course. Owned by a German count ... Can't remember his name."

"A baron, actually. Hans Von Kempelen."

"Yes, that's him."

"The baron thought he'd establish a town, as you do when you have money to spare, and decided the best way to lure buyers for lots was to build a pleasure palace. And that's what he did, calling it the Lenore Casino. Named it after his late wife."

Cash was struck by the similarity of name, very similar to his Lenora's. It must be nice, to build a place for your loved one: though it was in memory of the baron's wife. Happily, Lenora was very much alive, as she ably proved only last night.

Berenice's soft gentle voice intruded on his pleasant warm thoughts. "It seemed attractive to my brother, though I argued against getting involved." She sniffed. "He withdrew money for a down-payment and took the train—"

"And he's gone missing, you say," Cash interrupted. "When did he set out?"

"Two weeks ago." Berenice's eyes glistened but she held his gaze. "I haven't heard from him since he left. I was becoming frantic with worry so I wired Devon, in the hope that he could investigate."

"Two weeks is a long time," Cash observed. "I don't suppose we know if he even arrived in Rock Springs or Green River?" Both fledgling cities were stops on the U.P. railroad.

Berenice's lips trembled. "I do … I do believe he must have arrived. After I pressed him, our bank manager told me that Horace wired for an additional withdrawal of $50,000."

Inwardly, Cash groaned. "Was it sent?"

"Yes. He supplied the agreed confirmation of identity."

"Do you know what that confirmation entails?"

"No. Only Horace and the bank manager know. I have my own, as well. It is normal practice when dealing with large sums of money that are transmitted around the country or even abroad."

"Isn't technology wonderful?" Cash mused. Not expecting an answer, he went on, "It seems to have come as a surprise to you; is there any reason why Horace didn't let you know about this withdrawal?"

She shook her head and the silver earrings glinted. "I can't think of any reason. We've always been close. And of course since our inheritance we've both been involved in the business finances."

"Has Horace access to your share of the inheritance?"

"No."

"That's good to hear."

"What do you mean, Mr. Laramie?"

"It's always possible that your brother has been coerced into withdrawing those extra funds."

She paled, her mouth opening in shock. "Oh, my God, no!"

"My dear," Penn said, "it is a possibility we must consider. There are many unscrupulous men in the world."

"I know, but … the baron …"

Penn raised a hand. "It may have nothing to do with the baron. Indeed, it is unwise to speculate at this stage. Let Cash investigate and he can report back to me and I to you."

She turned in her chair, faced Cash, and said, her tone adamant, "No, Devon, that will not do at all. I must go with you, Mr. Laramie."

Penn exchanged a pained look with Cash.

"I insist," Berenice added.

Cash stood, passing the brim of his hat through his hands. "Have you traveled much, Berenice? Can you ride?"

"My brother went by train."

"Yes, but Lenore Casino is quite a ways outside Rock Springs, about a day's ride. I'll be taking my horse. If you're not up to it, I'd suggest …"

Abruptly, Berenice stood, her cheeks flushed. "I can ride as well as any man, Marshal. In fact, I'm better than my brother in that regard!"

"All right. Have you a horse?"

"No, but I can get one soon enough." She hefted her reticule. "I have the means."

Cash appraised her from head to toe and nodded. "You sure do, Berenice."

Chuckling, Penn stood. "I can see you both are going to get on nicely. You might even make a good team!"

Cash darted a glare.

"Just joking, Cash." He added an aside to Berenice, "The only partner he seems comfortable working with is a fellow U.S. Marshal, Miles."

"Comfortable," Cash retorted. "We've saved each other's life more than once. Comfortable doesn't cut it."

"Maybe so. Anyway, as it happens you might come across Miles out that way. He's gone to Fort Bridger."

"Surely he's not enlisting?"

Penn grinned. "Hardly! No, he's picking up a suspected murderer and bringing him here for trial."

CHAPTER TWO

RAVEN

Fort Bridger was unlike most forts Miles had been in; this one had no outer defensive wall, relying on the number of troops stationed here. The stone buildings had seen better days, he reckoned.

"Well, I've seen everything now, a black marshal with his black prisoner!" snapped a bearded sergeant as Miles escorted the chained detainee to the Major's office on the opposite side of the fort's parade ground. "Trial's too good for the bastard!"

"Ignore him," said Vincent Raven, shuffling with dignity despite the chains at his ankles.

Miles ignored Raven and spun on his heel, rounded on the sergeant. "A man's innocent until a court of law proves him guilty!"

About to retort, the soldier must have thought better of it on seeing the depth of feeling in the lawman's brown eyes. Muttering into his beard, he stalked off.

Miles stepped onto the boardwalk, opened the door and the pair of them entered the building.

An adjutant rose to his feet behind his desk. "Major Sanders is ready for you, Marshal."

Miles removed his hat. "Keep an eye on my prisoner, soldier."

"Sure, sir."

Miles rapped his knuckles on the door labeled *Camp Commander*, opened it and entered.

Major Jonathan Harrison sat behind his desk; its surface was cluttered with papers. "You have your prisoner, Marshal?" He gestured at a chair.

"Yes, Major." Miles sat facing him. "I'll leave with him first light tomorrow."

The bugler sounded Supper Call.

The major leaned forward. "Yet you have him outside, I hear."

"I'd like to remove his shackles and share a meal with him."

"Isn't that unorthodox?"

"Mr. Raven has given his word he won't escape. Besides, once he has eaten, I'll handcuff him for the night."

"And where will you stay tonight?"

"In the stable."

"Why there? Your smart attire doesn't seem appropriate for sleeping rough."

"I can soon shine my boots, if I need to, sir."

The major didn't register the sarcasm. "We have an adequate guardhouse; it's been Raven's abode since he was brought in."

"The livery will be safer. There seems a lot of bad feeling about him in your fort, Major."

"I trust you're not suggesting that anything fatal will befall Mr. Raven."

"Not at all, sir. But I don't want to break a few bigoted skulls unless I'm forced ..."

Major Harrison studied Miles, and then slowly smiled. "I take your meaning."

"Are you aware of Raven's past, sir?"

"A little. He's ex-ninth cavalry. He's knowledge-able about horse flesh and is now a horse-wrangler."

"That's right. I checked on him before I left Cheyenne. The murder is out of character; he was a good soldier in the ninth. He served in D Troop under Capt. Francis Dodge and was mentioned in despatches after the end of the Milk River siege with renegade Utes."

"I heard about that, but the evidence seems damning, Marshal."

"Isn't it a mite circumstantial?"

"I thought your remit was to transport the prisoner for trial, not to investigate the crime."

Miles shrugged. "Just curious, is all."

"Well, sadly for Raven, he was found in the town's post office standing over the slain postmaster, Mr. Edgar Clemm. Packets of opium were strewn about. He denies it, naturally, but the postmaster was still warm, according to a lawyer, Rufus Wilmot, who entered moments later. Sheriff Arnold Royster brought Raven here for protective custody, before he could be lynched. There's bad feeling about him in the town, as well; Mr. Clemm was a greatly liked citizen of Green River."

* * *

In the buttery light of the stable's kerosene lantern, Miles fed a carrot to his pinto. Raven sat on a bale of hay to his right, a wrist handcuffed to a metal rail separating one stall from another. An empty food plate and a fork lay on another bale.

"As I told you, I'm black, Marshal, so I'll get no justice."

Miles turned. "Utter hogwash!" He stroked his stubble. "I certainly don't judge a man by his color, only by what he does with his life. Judge Benton's the same. He makes his pronouncements according to the evidence."

Raven laughed mirthlessly. "Judges, lawyers! They're all the same!"

"You need to stop bundling folk into straitjacket categories, Mr. Raven. We're all individuals. The sooner you learn that, the better."

"But the lawyer as good as says I did it. It's my word against his. A lawyer, for cryin' out loud!"

"Who're they going to believe? There's no definite evidence."

"Well, I knelt by Mr. Clemm—he'd been stabbed—but I couldn't help him, he was dead—"

"And I suppose you got blood on your clothes while being all helpful and neighborly?"

"I don't like your tone, Marshal."

"Wait till you get in court. The prosecutor's tone will be a lot worse."

"Maybe so." He pulled a pipe from his pocket and then chewed on the stem. "Yeah, to answer your question, I'd just got to my feet when the lawyer walked in. He let out a hue and cry and before I could explain anything I was arrested by the sheriff and brung here and put in the guardhouse."

"You're also accused of a lesser crime, trading in opium—supplying the Chinese coal miners of Rock Springs."

"I don't know why they bothered with that, untrue as it is. I'll hang for the murder. They can't hang me twice."

"They'll use it to blacken your character, Mr. Raven."

"Yeah, right. As if I ain't black enough, eh?"

Miles chuckled at that and then threw him a small pouch of Bull Durham.

"You know, Marshal, I wouldn't touch that stuff. I don't even drink alcohol. I've seen what it can do to even the strongest of men." He tamped tobacco into his pipe's bowl. "And my wife Gwendolyn won't think kindly if I imbibed."

Miles was intrigued. It shouldn't be difficult to verify Raven's statement of abstinence. "Where's your wife now?"

"Bryan, watching over twenty horses."

"The ghost town?"

"Yeah." Miles lit Raven's pipe. Raven puffed for a while, then added, "I set up a corral and we've been trading from there. I was going to send a wire to a buyer in Laramie. He wanted eight mounts."

"Does your wife know you've been arrested?"

Raven lowered his gaze to the floor. "I doubt it. She's probably worried sick right now. You see, we keep to ourselves, only going into town for supplies; sometimes we go to Green River, sometimes to Rock Springs, so we're not that well known."

"That's unfortunate. I'll think on that. Have you made a written statement?"

"Sure. The fort commander has it."

"Okay, I'll take it with us. I've brought a horse for you. We'll travel by train to Green River and I'll make enquiries there before going on. And I'll also make a report on anything I learn."

"Should be a small report, then, Marshal."

"Stay positive, Mr. Raven."

CHAPTER THREE

AN AFFRAY FOR FREY

Cash was surprised to find Berenice waiting for him at the agreed time outside her hotel. She was astride a handsome chestnut and wore a calico split riding skirt, matching jacket and a white linen blouse. Her broad-brimmed hat was also calico. He noticed that there was an 1873 Winchester snug in its boot and the saddle was well worn, complete with bulging saddle-bags. Beside her was a piebald loaded with her two carpetbags. "You acquired your horses and equipment without much delay, I see, Berenice."

She wafted a hand; her gloves were pristine kid leather. "I won it all in a poker game last night, actually."

He laughed. "Remind me not to risk a game of chance with you."

"I don't gamble with friends—it's one way to lose them."

He doffed his hat. "Glad you consider me your friend." He nodded at the rifle. "Can you use that?"

She jutted out her chin. "I surely can."

"Better than your brother, I take it?"

Her cheeks dimpled in amusement. "We had a competitive childhood."

They set off down the broad main street to the rail station. She was a good rider and gave the impression of being quite comfortable in the saddle, and trailed the spare horse with ease. When he commented on the amount of luggage, she replied, "It's stuff I might need for the journey."

He'd explained that the distance from Cheyenne to Rock Springs was almost three hundred miles and would have taken them about seven days by horse. "So, it makes sense to travel by train and take the horses."

"Well, of course it does, Marshal," she responded. "It saves time as well. We need to find Horace before his trail goes cold."

He feared that any trail Horace Rohmer might have left would be exceedingly cold by now.

She stood by while he led the horses up the ramp into the freight car. To one side in a locked cage he saw crates and baggage stacked up. About ten crates were labeled "slot machines." He handed over Berenice's bags to the freight man who exchanged them for a ticket.

Once the horses were settled and tethered with a bag of feed each, Cash descended the ramp and re-joined Berenice.

"Everything all right?" she asked.

He showed her the luggage ticket. "Bags safely stowed and the horses are comfortable. Your chestnut was a mite nervous at first. Probably hasn't traveled by train before."

"But he's fine now, Marshal?"

Cash nodded. "If I'm going to call you Berenice, you can call me Cash, okay?"

Her golden brown eyes shone at him. "Yes, of course, Cash."

"I'm glad that's resolved." He took her arm and they walked along the platform.

As they boarded the first class compartment, she raised an elegant eyebrow. "Claiming this on your expenses?"

"Expenses? I should be so lucky. I normally wouldn't travel first class but for your consideration, I thought it more appropriate."

"Don't go out of your way on my account, Cash."

They settled into a double seat, their backs to the engine, "So I can see where we've been," she stated. The seats were cramped, his broad shoulders pressing against her more delicate frame.

A man on the other side of the aisle gave Cash a quizzical look, but said nothing. He was short, with dark brown eyes and thin hay-colored hair with stray wisps over his prominent ears, a blond moustache and thick eyebrows.

"Hey, are you a real U.S. Marshal?" he said, more an exclamation than a question.

"That's what the badge says," Cash remarked good-humoredly.

The man wiped his palm on the chest of his checked jacket and then leaned over, offering his hand. "Name's

Willard Frey, purveyor of precision machines manufactured in Chicago!"

Pointing toward the rear of the carriage, Cash said, "Those crates of slot machines are yours?"

"That's right, Marshal!" He persisted in exclaiming each sentence. Cash wondered how he'd express himself if in distress. "I'm taking my wares to Baron von Kempelen's casino!"

"Then you're in the right carriage," Cash observed, indicating further down the aisle an attractive woman at a table with three men. They were playing poker and she was dealing the cards.

Berenice chuckled and covered her mouth with her gloved hand.

Frey laughed. "That's Poker Jane! I wouldn't trust my luck against her!"

"Or I against your slot machines?" Cash suggested.

"Touché, sir!"

Frey was still chuckling seconds later when two swarthy men entered the carriage, guns drawn.

"This is a hold-up," said the tall one with a patch over one eye. "Be generous, folks!"

His bald companion, shorter with narrow eyes, chuckled, while passing his hat round for valuables. "We have a conscience. We only rob those in first class."

"Mighty considerate of you," Cash said under his breath. He noticed that Berenice didn't seem alarmed at all. She was full of surprises.

Willard Frey leaned into the aisle and began, "Look here, this is a Marsh—"

Cash swiftly swung his leg across the aisle and kicked the salesman. Giving him a warning glare, he covered his badge with his jacket.

Shortly, Eyepatch approached their seat and leered at Berenice. "Sorry, ma'am, but our need is greater than yours. Hand over your finery. You as well, buster," he added, jerking his pistol at Cash.

"One moment, sir." Berenice delved in her reticule, unexpectedly pulled out a derringer, and fired at the man's chest.

In the same instant, Cash rose to his feet, drew his Colt and shoved the dead Eyepatch to one side.

The bald robber snarled, "You're dead meat!"

"Wouldn't you like to think so!" Cash replied, firing his Colt.

The bald robber stumbled forward, shooting into the floor, and dropped his overflowing hat.

A third man entered the carriage, gun drawn. "What the hell?"

"That's where you're bound!" Cash said and fired again.

CHAPTER FOUR

WILMOT

While Raven slept well, despite his handcuffed situation, Miles had a restless night, plagued by thoughts of innocent men climbing the gallows. He woke tired.

He shook Raven and they mounted as Reveille sounded.

"We'll grab a bite to eat at the rail station," Miles said.

They rode out of the fort and headed toward the railroad.

The train journey was brief, since it only covered about sixty miles to the town of Green River. They alighted from the train and Miles led their horses down the ramp.

Shortly, they rode to the livery stable where Miles came to an agreement with the stableman for them to stay for the day and overnight. "There's plenty of lodgings to be had here," the man had said with civic pride.

"I don't want to advertise the fact that I have a prisoner," Miles explained.

"Suits me fine, Marshal. A little extra money from you won't go amiss."

The stableman left briefly to bring a plate of food for Raven.

"While you kill time, Mr. Raven, I'll let the sheriff know I'm here with you. Maybe I can make enquiries in town as well, see if I can turn up anything." He tightened the cinch on his horse.

Raven offered a brief faint smile. "Thank you, though I doubt if you will find the real culprit. No offence, but there are no clues." He peered at the beams in the stable's ceiling. "I'm going to hang, for sure, I know I am."

"Only if you're guilty, Mr. Raven. Tomorrow, we'll set out for Bryan to let your wife know what's happened." He took the reins and led his horse to the stable door.

"Thanks, Marshal, I appreciate that. It'll be good to get some fresh air—while I can ..."

Miles paused at the door, more convinced than ever that Raven was innocent.

* * *

Green River's wide street and false-fronted buildings were dominated by an enormous butte that over-shadowed the green water of the river. Several men and women walked about, intent on their own business. Miles smelled cooked food and his stomach rumbled as he rode past a lodging house, the meat market and a saloon and reached the hitching post in front of the adjacent sheriff's office. He dismounted, fastened the reins and stepped onto the boardwalk.

A sudden commotion erupted from the saloon and a Chinese man tumbled through the batwing doors. He stumbled and then fell into the dust.

Three men emerged from the saloon, all of them swaying and worse for drink, fists cocked. A tall bulk of a man, a short fellow and a wiry man.

The Chinaman's prominent cheeks and forehead were bruised. He regained his feet and dusted himself down. He stood, ready to fight, though his hands were rigid and flat, not curled into bare knuckles like his opponents.

Plucky little fellow, Miles thought.

"Hey, you three, I don't like the odds here," Miles called. He moved closer. "Care to take us both on?"

The bulkier one swore and barreled off the board-walk, charging straight for Miles.

Turning so his right side faced the man, Miles waited and then gauged it perfectly, thrusting out his boot sideways, directly into the man's midriff. The blow stopped him immediately.

Miles saw the Chinaman swiftly counter the short man's punches and deflect the wiry man's blows with the edge of his hands in a blur of motion. He distinctly heard a collar-bone crack and in the same moment the wiry man uttered a shout of extreme agony and pulled his revolver. Miles drew and fired, the bullet catching him in the bicep of his gun-arm. The Chinaman deftly disarmed the wounded man and knocked the short man to the ground.

"What's going on here?" barked the sheriff, running over, his nickel-plated Colt Single Action Army revolver drawn. He gestured with the barrel at Miles. "Put that away, Mister!"

As Miles holstered his gun, the bulky man stood slightly doubled up, supporting himself against the boardwalk post. "This black card-sharp—he set on us, sheriff. We didn't stand a chance!"

The sheriff wore a low-slung Buscadero gun rig. He removed his off-white Stetson and raised an eyebrow at Miles.

"I ain't any card-sharp. I like to dress smart." Peeling back his coat, Miles displayed his badge.

The sheriff whistled. "A Negro U.S. Marshal, eh? Welcome to my town!" He turned to the three men; all of them seemed to feel sorry for themselves, and with good reason. "I've told you before, Frank Behen, stop bullying the Chinamen!"

"But—but sheriff," wailed the wounded wiry man, "he shot me. I can't work now!"

"You shouldn't have drawn your gun just because you couldn't best your opponent in a fist fight," Miles said.

"What fist?" the wiry man snapped.

He had a point, Miles allowed.

"The Chinaman broke my collarbone!" wailed the short one.

"O'Donnell, Brosnan, go see the doc," the sheriff said. Then he faced Behen. "As for you, if I have any more trouble from you, I'll get the foreman to fire you!"

Behen glared and growled, "I'll get even with you, Marshal!"

"That's not a good idea," the sheriff said.

Accompanying the two hurt men, Behen stumbled off.

The Chinaman walked up to Miles and bowed slightly, and said in faltering English, "Thank you."

"Glad to help. Though I reckon you were quite capable of handling those two guys."

The Chinaman grinned and bowed again and then melted into the shadows at the side of the saloon.

"Damned coalminers!" moaned the sheriff in an aside.

"I'm glad I caught you, sheriff. I wanted to talk to you about Mr. Raven. He's my prisoner and I'll be taking him to Cheyenne tomorrow."

* * *

Sheriff Arnold Royster poured coffee. "It's as the fort commander says, Marshal Miles. Mr. Wilmot walked in and found Vince Raven standing over Edgar Clemm's body."

"How did you get involved so quickly?"

"Wilmot ducked his head out the door and called 'murder' and then waylaid a young lad to come get me."

Miles filled his pipe and lit it, mulling over the information. "Did Mr. Wilmot touch anything?"

"No. He stood by the door, adamant that Vince wouldn't get away."

"What about a rear entrance?"

Sheriff Royster shrugged. "Yeah, there is one. But he never thought about it, I guess. And Vince didn't consider running off anyway. When I got there, he said he found the body like that."

"Don't you think it was odd for Mr. Raven to stay around, if he had killed the postmaster?"

"Sure. If I'd done the deed, I'd've hightailed it out of town."

"But the evidence of the blood on him suggested his guilt?"

"Yes. And the postmaster's body was still warm when I got there."

Miles studied the clock on the wall. "Do you reckon I'll be able to catch Mr. Wilmot in his office?"

"I should think so. He doesn't stop for lunch, that one."

* * *

Although the shingle gave the hours of Mr. Rufus Wilmot, Attorney at Law as 9am-2pm; 4pm-6pm, the office windows still glowed yellow, so he was in during the lunch period.

Miles rapped the butt of his gun on the door, then holstered it.

After a short interval a white-bearded man in his mid-fifties opened the door. His white bushy eyebrows lifted and his grey eyes pierced. "Yes?"

"Marshal Gideon Miles, sir." He lifted back his jacket to reveal his badge.

"How can I help you, Marshal?" He pulled a fob watch from his suit vest pocket; his pants were tight, due to a paunch that had outgrown the suit. "I was thinking of stopping for a bite to eat."

"This will only take a minute of your time, Mr. Wilmot "

Wilmot heaved a sigh. "Very well. Come in."

The office was dark, even though it was about mid-day. A kerosene lantern illuminated the place and the dust. Every surface was cluttered with books, rolls of papers, ribbons and seals. Miles didn't wait to be asked but found a chair, removed a stack of books and placed them on the carpet, and then sat.

"Make yourself at home, why don't you?" Wilmot sat behind his disorganized desk.

Miles explained his purpose for the visit.

"You are to be commended; that's most assiduous of you, Marshal." He projected an urbane, pleasant manner. "I only wish I'd arrived at the post office a few minutes earlier, perhaps I could have prevented the tragedy—or at least I might have actually witnessed Raven committing the dastardly act."

"Why were you in the post office, Mr. Wilmot?"

"I … I was—in fact, I still am—waiting for a set of legal papers. They were mailed to me from New York. Should have been here by now. Quite frustrating, actually "

"Yeah, I'm sure. Mail can be so unreliable."

"Indeed! I'm only sorry I couldn't be of more help. I suppose Raven will hang for his crime?"

"Only if he's guilty, sir."

"You mean there's some doubt? I'd have thought my testimony placed him at the scene, and his blood-stained clothing condemned him."

"In my long career I've known many a man who has happened to be at the wrong place at the wrong time—and often as not he's been innocent."

"But that would mean the murderer is still abroad, no?"

"Could be. I surmise that the postmaster was slain in connection to the opium. That may be a trail worth investigating, I reckon." He stood. "Any place you'd recommend for a bite to eat, Mr. Wilmot?"

"Ma Brewster's eatery is adequate, Marshal."

"Do you eat there?"

"Sometimes. But today I'm going to The Bells hotel. Out of town."

"Well, thank you for your time. Good day, Mr. Wilmot."

CHAPTER FIVE

THE BELLS

The train arrived at Rock Springs in the evening. Passengers who were traveling further dashed off to grab food and drink at the concession on the platform.

Cash helped Berenice onto the platform and they then went to the freight carriage. She waited at the foot of the ramp.

He paid little notice to the three corpses covered by tarpaulins and laid against the wall next to the luggage cages. Quite sanguine about their fate, he gave the freight man his luggage ticket, picked up Berenice's carpetbags, fastened them to the piebald and then led the three horses down the ramp.

Berenice's cheeks were aglow, and she was pleased to see her chestnut and mounted unaided.

The conductor rushed to Cash's side. "Marshal, what about the bodies of the desperados?"

"Contact the sheriff …"

"But we only stop here for fifteen minutes!"

"... at your destination." Cash produced a sheet of paper, which Berenice had signed as a witness. "This report will advise the lawman there of the facts and he can arrange for the burials." He bit off the end of a cheroot, lit it. "He might want to check the wanted dodgers; he's welcome to any reward."

"Yes, sir ..."

Mounting up, Cash said, "We're going to the livery stable now. If you have any more questions before you leave, you'll find us there."

"Okay, Marshal."

The livery man at the station remembered Horace. "Couldn't mistake all that red hair, Marshal." He turned to Berenice. "He was a real gent. Staying at *The Bells*, he said." The man scratched his head. "Mr. Rohmer didn't say how long he'd want the horse. But he paid me so well I ain't troubled about his absence yet."

"Well, I am, sir," Berenice said.

Willard Frey sauntered in. "I need to hire a buckboard!" he exclaimed.

"Anything else you want to know?" the livery man asked Cash, hesitant, clearly eager to attend to a client.

Tears glistened in Berenice's eyes. "Marshal, please. We need to get on."

"Thanks, Mister." Cash passed the livery man a tip. Acknowledging Frey, he said, "Good luck with your crates."

"Thanks, Marshal. See you around, maybe!"

* * *

A short ride to the outskirts of the town brought them to the hotel called *The Bells*. It was on a slight rise, commanding a good view, a grand building constructed of clapboard, stone and tile, with two turrets on the south and north side; imposing, in a kind of splendid isolation. A short distance away was an undertaker's, a chapel and a graveyard.

"Why build the hotel here?" Berenice asked.

"Maybe they expected the town to grow and eventually surround it?"

"But the rail line ruined that idea, it seems."

"Seems so. Doubtless we'll have more than enough rooms to choose from!"

They dismounted at the hitching post to the right of the entrance steps, and walked into the foyer together. Cash was immediately struck by a strong sweet-smelling odor.

"Joss sticks," Berenice observed.

"Yeah, you're right."

The reception desk was immediately in front; a flight of stairs curved from the right-hand side to a gallery that led off to rooms and a passageway. On the left was a double door with a sign indicating it was the dining room. Next to it was the guest lounge; he glimpsed a huge unlit inglenook fireplace; and next to that, a door to the kitchen.

A diminutive Chinese woman mopped the tiled floor.

Behind the reception counter stood a woman in her late thirties. She was busy writing in a large ledger. She wore very fine clothing, a flowing black lace dress with a tight bodice. As they approached, she looked up and raised a hand to adjust a stray strand of black hair; the rest was tied in a bun. She smiled. "Welcome!" She swiveled round the register to face them; it was a virgin fresh double page spread. "I'm the joint owner of this establishment. Madeline Allan at your service." She dipped a pen in the countersunk inkpot and held it out to Cash.

"Hello," Cash said, scrawling his name and occupation. "We'd like two separate rooms, please."

She studied him pointedly. He was surprised to note that her left eye was green while her right was blue. "Of course. Only the best for a U.S. Marshal." She could read upside down.

"Are we too late for a meal?" Berenice asked, writing her name.

"No, I can rustle up something, ma'am. I'll give you a menu, when we've completed your registration." Her mouth gaped briefly as she dabbed the entries with a small sheet of blotting paper. "Oh, Miss Berenice Rohmer?"

"Yes?"

"Are you related to Mr. Horace Rohmer?"

Berenice nodded. "He's my brother."

Cash turned the page, found the earlier entry for Horace Rohmer. Arrival date, then a week later, the departure date five days ago. He applied his memory and decided that Horace left on the day the extra withdrawal took place.

He eyed Berenice. She'd noticed as well.

A black cat sauntered next to Berenice and slid its body around her feet, purring, its bright green eyes scrutinizing her.

"Oh, don't mind Pluto," Madeline Allan said. "I'm surprised, though, as it's unusual for him to take to strangers. He clearly likes you, Miss."

"An unusual name," Cash remarked.

"A fanciful idea of my brother's. Named after the god of the underworld."

"Better than Hades, anyway," Berenice supplemented, stroking the cat.

"Welcome!" enthused a man dressed in black who descended the stairs. He was gaunt, with an ashen complexion and a hooked nose. He wore a cream shirt and cravat and a multi-hued vest. "I see you've met our feline mascot!" He brushed black long hair away from his ears and extended a hand. "Roderick Allan, joint proprietor. Pleased to meet you, Marshal." His hands were soft, the fingers long, the nails bitten. His left eye was blue, the right green.

"Thanks for the personal welcome, Mr. Allan." He arched an eyebrow. "Are you twins by any chance?"

Roderick Allan chuckled. "Precisely! I'm the eldest by an hour, apparently."

"Roderick, Miss Berenice here is Mr. Rohmer's sister!"

"How splendid!" Roderick cocked his head to one side. "But not twins?"

"No, sir. Horace is three years my senior."

"I remember your brother well. A gentleman, a charming man. I was sorry he cut short his stay with us."

Berenice wrung her hands. "Do you know what his plans were after he left?"

"Indeed I do, Miss. He said he was going on to stay with Baron von Kempelen." Roderick gestured vaguely at the entrance doors. "At the Lenore Casino. He had business there, apparently."

"How far is the baron's place?" Cash asked.

"His spread is quite vast, sir. But if you mean the Casino, it is a good thirty miles round trip from here."

"Thanks. I'd like to arrange for the horses—you have a stable-hand?"

"Of course, Marshal. Leave it to me. The stables are at the back, with a good-sized corral too."

Cash turned to Berenice. "It's too late to go now. As I'd thought, the casino's a good day's ride."

Before Berenice could reply, Madeline Allan said, "If I may, Miss, I would like to offer you the same room your brother occupied."

Cash waylaid a curious glance between the two siblings, but Roderick didn't speak.

"It offers a splendid view," Madeline continued, ringing the desk bell.

"Why, that is kind of you," Berenice said. "Thank you, Miss Allan."

A young Chinese man appeared from the room behind the reception desk. He was given the room keys and picked up Berenice's bags. Cash carried his Yellow Boy rifle and slung his saddlebags over his shoulder.

As Mr. Allan led them to the staircase, Cash said, "Did you happen to know if Mr. Rohmer spoke to any of your guests? Did you overhear any conversations he might have had?"

"No, I'm sorry, Marshal. Our guests tend to keep to themselves. My sister and I are not in the habit of listening in to our clientele's discussions. I must admit that Mr. Rohmer tended to be quite preoccupied and didn't mix with our other guests."

On the wall at the head of the stairs was a fire-axe and below it a bucket of sand, the proprietors' limited concession to safety. "Had he been to see the baron before he finally left here?" Berenice asked.

"That is my understanding, yes," Roderick said. "Not long after that, he made a visit to town, and then signed out. I must admit I thought his departure was abrupt .... Ah, here we are."

The Chinese porter unlocked the first door and opened it and carried Berenice's bags in. It was a compact room with a double bed, a wardrobe, a tallboy with a washbasin and towel, and a square of thin carpet. The walls were covered with deep red flock paper. The window, draped with matching red curtains, presented a view of the butte's dark silhouette. Despite the pervading aroma from joss-sticks, the room had a distinct smell about it; new paint, Cash reckoned.

"Has it been recently decorated?" Berenice enquired.

"How observant of you, Miss!" Roderick said. "Yes, we try to maintain standards."

Berenice gazed out the window, and Cash looked over her shoulder. The land undulated, ochre dotted with wild flowers, and purple hills shimmered in the near-distance. "Your wife's right, Mr. Allan, it's a splendid view," Berenice said.

They left her to freshen herself for dinner and Cash was led to his room, which the Chinese porter opened then gave him the key. It was similarly appointed but had not been recently decorated, so perhaps those standards had slipped a mite. It was hospitable enough, he thought.

* * *

Miles reckoned the ride to Rock Springs was about eighteen miles or so, and he was content to take it easy after filling up with beef stew and an apple pie from Ma Brewster's.

He rode at a good pace and passed a fork in the road with a sign-post indicating 'The Bells Hotel, Price Funeral Parlor, chapel and cemetery.'

He stuck to the main track, however, and two hours later, his horse finally cantered past the Union Pacific sign into the coal mine complex outside the township.

Dusk brushed the sky and work had stopped. He steered his horse through a tent village on the periphery of the mine workings.

People strolled here and there, chatting, smoking, laughing, joking, miners of all kinds, though the majority seemed to be Chinese.

Camp-fires glowed. He caught the tantalizing smell of food and his stomach rumbled.

He passed a big black tent, where two heavy-set Chinese men stood guard at the entry flap.

Further ahead, signposted, was his destination, a wooden shack labeled *Mine Foreman.*

Rance Nuffield was almost the same height as Miles, but stockier and in his forties. He was welcoming but didn't offer a smile or a handshake as he led Miles into the shack. He took a seat and indicated a chair. "I'm troubled, Marshal."

"The opium, Mr. Nuffield?"

"Partly that. There's no way I can control it, there are too many involved, and it's a cultural thing, I guess. The celestials seem to have a weakness for the stuff." Miles had heard Chinese called Chinks and Celestials, two of the more polite monikers. "But when the drug affects men who then die in an accident, then it becomes my business."

"Good to know you care about your men."

"Hell, they're cheap labor—but they've been trained. So every man who dies in an accident means we have to train another one. And sometimes the accidents delay the mining process."

You're all heart, Miles amended to himself. "You said 'partly.' What else is troubling you?"

"Anti-Chinese feeling is getting mighty raw lately."

"The Chinese Exclusion Act's been around about three years now—suspending Chinese immigration for ten years."

"Yeah, but there are already thousands of them in the country, and naturally we're going to employ them: they're cheap, as I said. But I'm beginning to wonder if something's brewing. The Rock Springs chapter of the Knights of Labor is rebel rousing. Can't you stop them, Marshal? We should be able to hire whoever we like— and not be dictated to by any organization."

"As I see it, there hasn't been any offense committed. Voicing a grievance is legitimate, Mr. Nuffield. People shouldn't be punished for forming an opinion. I'd hate to think that would ever come to pass."

"Talk is cheap as well, Marshal, but it can get expensive if it stirs up trouble."

"Anyone in particular you recommend I talk to?"

"Frank Behen is the loudest talker of them."

Miles nodded. "I came across him in town earlier. Yes, he sounds like a rebel-rouser."

"You can say that again!"

"As I've said, I can't do anything about men blustering, even unsavory Behen. If they advocate violence, then that's a different thing entirely. No, I meant concerning the opium. I want to know who profits from it."

"David Chang speaks good English. I go to him if I have a problem with the celestials. He might be able to help."

CHAPTER SIX

AMONTILLADO

As Cash and Berenice settled at their table in the dining room, Mr. Allan approached and handed them the menu. He seemed to only have eyes for Berenice, which wasn't surprising, since she appeared very desirable in her blue satin dress, two white lace petticoats peeking from the bottom, her lace-trimmed bodice exposing a generous cleft between her breasts. Cash felt under-dressed; he'd changed into a fresh black linen shirt and combed his hair.

Mr. Allan pointed at a man with a long twirling moustache, sitting at a table adjacent to Willard Frey, the slot machine salesman. "That is Monsieur Valdemar. He supplies us with wines from the continent of Europe. We pride ourselves on our outstanding cellar." He gestured at the drinks trolley, crammed with assorted bottles of different colors, shapes and sizes.

"Really?" Cash said.

Mr. Allan bobbed his head with enthusiasm. "We have an exquisite sherry. Amontillado." He reached over to the trolley, produced the dark bottle. Smiling unctuously at Berenice, he added, "May I recommend it as an apéritif, Miss?"

"Yes, thank you," Berenice said, "I that would be lovely."

"No, thanks," Cash replied. "I'll stick with beer."

Turning up his nose slightly, Mr. Allan said, "As you wish, sir."

Berenice scanned the menu. "And do you have a merlot? I think the little blackbird would suit the rabbit."

"Blackbird?" Cash queried.

"Merlot is French for 'the little blackbird'," she explained.

"Oh, *mais oui!*" enthused Mr. Allan. "Impeccable taste, Miss."

"I'll have chicken," Cash decided.

"Yes, of course you would, sir. And to begin, Miss, a beef consommé?"

"Yes, thank you."

"I'll have the soup," Cash ordered.

"Yes, of course, sir."

"With fresh bread," Cash added.

"Naturally, all our bread is freshly baked on the premises, sir." Haughtily, Mr. Allan strode off toward the kitchen.

The hotel boasted two more couples and, besides the salesman Frey, four men at separate tables, all served by Chinese waiters. Not a thriving business, but getting by, presumably. All the guests seemed to keep to themselves, as Cash hadn't seen them about the hotel or grounds, only in here.

At the outset, Berenice commented, "There seem to be a lot of Chinese staff."

"There are a lot round about here. They're cheap labor, Berenice. They keep quiet, just work and mind their own business."

She reminisced about her childhood in Boston with Horace They'd had a close happy childhood, with loving parents who were now sadly both deceased. But she didn't dwell on their deaths. "They had a good life and had plenty of love in it, which many can't say."

"That's true," Cash agreed. "Live your life well. It's the only one you get."

"That sounds like a toast." They clinked glasses.

Cash found the meal surprisingly palatable, and the alcohol went down very smoothly. While he smoked a cheroot at the table, Berenice sipped her black coffee.

Willard Frey approached them diffidently. "Sorry to butt in like this! I heard the proprietors say you're going to the Lenore Casino! It's a long ride, so I'd welcome the company. The buckboard's already loaded for an early start. I reckon the baron will be pleased with the machines. Do you fancy going with me?"

"Sure," Cash replied. "We can meet here at seven, and leave after breakfast."

"Seven it is, then. And that's a lucky number, you know?"

"Really? How fascinating!" Berenice said and raised a puzzled eyebrow as Cash glared at her.

"Lady Luck has taken a shine to me, Miss," Frey went on. "I was in the right place at the right time. Chicago, it was. I happened on a manufacturer of slot machines. I could see they'd be popular out here. They may only take nickels or pennies, but those little coins sure soon add up to sizeable takings!"

"And," Cash interposed, "I suppose the takings favor the manufacturer?"

"Or the owner of the machines. I call them one-armed bandits."

"Why is that?" Berenice asked.

Cash sighed. "Because the machines are operated by the gambler pulling a metal arm that cranks a variety of colorful wheels—depicting cards, or bells or even fruit. Line them up right and you win. But of course the machines are rigged so that they rob the gambler."

"Oh, I feel affronted, Marshal," Frey said good-humoredly. "Most gamblers worth their salt know the odds are stacked against them. That's what draws them on—to beat the system!"

"Wouldn't you like to think so? Since I've come across these 'one-armed bandits' I've found they're even more addictive than card-games."

"Addiction is a strong accusation, Marshal."

"People can spend their money how they like, Mr. Frey. Trouble is, when they lose it all, they're driven to crime to feed their addiction."

"I'd never thought about it like that," Frey mused. "Sadly," he added with a salesman's smile, "you can't stop progress!"

"The night progresses, as well," Cash said, standing. "That's all very interesting, but since we have an early start, I think we should catch some shut-eye." He held out a hand and Berenice took it and got to her feet.

"Yes, of course!" Frey said. "I'm sorry about rattling on so much! I get so excited when I talk about my 'bandits'!"

"Let's hope they're the only bandits on the trail tomorrow, Mr. Frey," Cash concluded.

They bid each other good night.

On their way up the stairs, Berenice chuckled and whispered, "I feared we'd never be rid of the poor man. All he thinks about is profit and games of chance!"

"Well, speaking from experience, Berenice, I've found life is one big gamble."

"Another wisecrack like that, Cash Laramie, and you can get on the next train back to Cheyenne!"

He grinned. "I like you when you're forceful."

"That's enough flippancy for one night," she chided.

"I promise to ration my flippancy from now on," he said as he led her to her door. "Sleep tight, Berenice."

She fumbled for her key in her reticule. "And you, Cash."

Despite the tedium of the journey, Cash found that he couldn't sleep tight or sober. A full moon shone into the room; he hadn't bothered drawing the curtains, since the window wasn't overlooked. He reached over to the bed-stand and lifted his fob watch. It was an hour or so since he'd removed his clothes and climbed into bed. He couldn't stop thinking about Berenice. She was quite a woman. Bold, independent, and very attractive.

A knock on his door intruded on his thoughts. He got out of bed, grabbed his Colt and padded across the floor, holding a pillow to cover himself.

"Who's there?" he called softly.

"It's me, Cash. I can't sleep … there's something in my room troubling me …"

He lowered the gun to the tallboy by the door and, awkwardly holding the pillow over his midriff, he unlocked and opened the door.

She was wearing a white cotton nightgown, and her red hair had been let down, draping over her shoulders. Her eyes reflected concern.

"What sort of something?"

She glanced up and down the corridor. "Can I come in?"

"Sure." He stepped aside, let her in and shut the door. "Scraping?" he queried, conscious of his state of undress. He felt foolish, clutching a pillow to his torso.

"Yes …" Her gaze dropped to the pillow and then raised sharply to his face, her cheeks flushed. "A kind of scratching sound behind the walls." She shuddered. "Rats, I imagine."

"Maybe that's why they redecorated, they had to fumigate the place …"

"… with joss-sticks? If so, maybe they didn't catch them all, perhaps?"

"Could be something like that. Do you want me to mosey along and check it out?"

She shook her head. "Not tonight. I'd rather stay here, if that's not too forward?"

"Sure." He clutched the pillow tightly. "I can always sleep in your room. Rats don't bother me none."

"No, please let me stay here with you tonight."

"Okay. I'll check your room tomorrow morning." He gestured with a nod. "I'll bunk on the floor."

"No, you won't, Mr. Laramie. That bed's big enough for the both of us."

Bold, independent, and very attractive? Sure. And forthright and determined—and a tempting woman.

CHAPTER SEVEN

GWENDOLYN

Miles sat outside a tent with David Chang who was half-Chinese, half-English. "Our men incessantly bicker," Chang said, "and gamble all the time, but they are not inclined to strike, and do not get drunk on payday or frequent the whorehouses."

"I'm sure the Chinese workers are a boon to the company," Miles said.

"Unlike some, they are not shy of work, either."

"What about smoking opium?"

"I try to root out those who fall prey to the poppy. It is not easy. They keep moving their den!"

"I'd have thought you'd be able to sniff them out, since it's a distinctive odor."

Chang laughed and looked around, sniffing the air. "Smell that? That's coal dust, trail dust, engine oil, cookfires burning …"

"I get your point." Miles thumbed over his shoulder. "I passed a black tent on my way in—two Chinese on guard."

"That is not an opium tent, Marshal. That is our meditation tent."

"Meditation. Really?"

"You sound dubious. I will take you."

Chang signed to the two men at the tent flap and they let Miles inside. There was a powerful smell of incense, but no opium odor. Eight barefoot men sat on mats, their legs crossed in oriental fashion, their wrists resting on their knees, faces composed, eyes shut. Outside noise penetrated faintly and the longer Miles watched, the more distant those sounds became. He was convinced he could hear the men breathing, and then their heart-beats, the inner silence was so profound and complete.

A gentle tug at his sleeve brought him back to reality. Chang led him outside and his senses were momentarily assaulted by the noise of people talking, walking, waggons rolling, dogs barking, and cats screeching.

Miles exhaled, surprised he'd been holding his breath. "That was instructive, but it doesn't help Mr. Raven, who's accused of trading in the stuff. Do you know how the opium gets into your men's hands?"

Chang shook his head. "The men who need the drug are cunning. I suspect that when I am away on an errand or some important task, certain items are exchanged behind my back."

"Certain items?"

"That could be gambling winnings, opium or simply extra or stolen food."

"At that moment, Miles recognized a Chinese man carrying a bucket of nails as he walked past a lamp. The man waved then ambled over. He spoke rapidly in Mandarin to Chang.

Chang turned to Miles. "This is Wang Feng. He says you're the man who stepped in when Behen, O'Donnell and Brosnan were bullying him."

"It was more than bullying, but yes, that was me."

Chang chuckled. "He was surprised that you recognized him."

"I don't see why he should be surprised."

"He says he's pleased. Most white men can't tell us apart."

Miles smiled ruefully. "I have that trouble with my color, too, it seems."

"I'll tell him that!" Chang said with a smile and proceeded to converse in Mandarin again.

"I wonder," Miles mused. "I'm still thinking about the source of the opium. Can you ask him if there is any white man who mixes with his fellows?"

"Yes, of course." Chang posited the question. The man nodded rapidly, giving a quick-fire response, gesturing vaguely at the tent village.

"Only the lawyer, he says," Chang translated. "He helps them with sending their money back home, arranges for official papers in the event of death, that sort of thing."

"What's the lawyer's name?"

"Rufus Wilmot."

"Well, fancy that." He shook Chang's hand. "Thanks, Mr. Chang, you've been most helpful." Miles bowed slightly to the Chinaman, whispered, "*Xie xie*," the only Chinese he knew: *thank you*. This was enough to raise a smile.

* * *

Cash woke refreshed at dawn and slipped out of bed while Berenice lay naked and serene on her back, her head surrounded by a halo of deep red hair, one leg bent, exposing her fiery bush. He pulled the sheet over her.

He stepped into his jeans and buttoned them up awkwardly, and then quietly padded out of the room, shut the door. The corridor wall lantern offered a wan glow; the passageway in semi-darkness and uninviting. He unlocked her door.

Inside, he stood and listened. A faint wisp of cool air blew through the small gap under the partially open sash window, fanned his bare torso. There was a very faint odor he'd associate with an outhouse, but the nearest toilet was at the end of the corridor.

He examined the skirting boards and floorboards around the edge of the room. There were no rat droppings, and no mouse-holes.

"Find anything?" Berenice asked, standing at the door, now wearing her nightdress.

He turned. Backlit from the corridor light, she presented a shapely silhouette, the cotton virtually see-through gauze.

He shook his head. "Whatever you'd heard, the cause is a mystery. Maybe the rats have gone elsewhere; besides, they're usually nocturnal creatures."

"Yes, of course. And that might account for the absence of any sound now."

He indicated her bags on the sideboard. "You're happy to come in to change?"

"Yes. It seems different in daylight. I do need to freshen up." She flushed.

"I'll give you a knock in twenty minutes and we can go for breakfast."

She chuckled. "And meet again dear Mr. Frey!"

A short while later he knocked and Berenice opened the door to him. She wore a simple green silk taffeta dress and a bodice that revealed her collar bones and shoulders, a tantalizing expanse of flesh that reminded him of their passionate night. She'd swept her hair under a small frilly bonnet. "Ready?"

She nodded and they went down to breakfast.

To Berenice's whispered pleasure, Willard Frey was not in evidence. After they'd ordered—egg over easy, bacon and beans for Cash, bread, butter and orange preserve for Berenice—Cash excused himself. "I'll check on the horses."

He made his way to the stables at the rear of the hotel. The stable-hand was cheerful and promised to prepare Cash's horse. He answered Cash's next query by pointing to Willard Frey's crates stacked on the buckboard. "I was just about ready to get the horse for Mr. Frey," he added.

Cash returned to the dining room, but Frey still hadn't appeared for breakfast.

A moment later, their food and coffee was brought on a large tray by Mr. Allan. Cash asked him about the salesman.

"Salesmen tend toward unpunctuality, I find, Marshal. I can arrange to have a member of staff knock on his room door?"

"No, don't trouble him. Our business is entirely separate. He seemed keen for my company for the long ride to Lenore Casino, that's all."

"You're going this morning, Marshal?

"Yes."

"And is Miss Rohmer accompanying you?"

"No. She can stay here until I send for her."

Berenice threw Cash a dark glare.

Mr. Allan didn't seem to notice the unspoken interchange between them. He poured the coffee. "That seems eminently sensible, Marshal." He bowed at Berenice. "We will certainly look after you, Miss, while the marshal is absent."

"I'm sure I'll appreciate that, Mr. Allan," she said and cut her slice of bread viciously.

* * *

After breakfast, neither spoke as they went up to his room. No sooner was the door shut than Berenice whirled round, her cheeks flushed red. "You can't seriously expect me to stay here while you go off to the casino!" she stormed.

"It's a long ride. Let me get the facts, Berenice. Then I can either send for you, or ..."

"Or what? Last night was immensely pleasurable, but you don't own me, Cash!"

He thought of Lenora and the exceedingly loose arrangement they enjoyed. "I don't hold with 'owning' any woman, Berenice. Truth is, I'm concerned about your brother's safety. I know you can handle yourself with that derringer—but really, I don't want you in jeopardy. Perhaps one Rohmer at risk is enough?"

"You really think Horace is at risk?"

Cash nodded. "I do. Carrying all that money was not a sensible move on his part."

"But nobody would know he carried it."

"Except the baron—and possibly his people?"

"Yes, that's highly likely," she conceded, her tone softening.

"And if Horace withdrew money wired to the bank, did anybody see him collect it?"

She blanched at that. "Oh, dear, yes, of course."

* * *

Miles and Raven left the livery straight after a breakfast of eggs, bacon and beans, having settled with the stableman. The ghost town of Bryan was to the north, mid-way between the townships of Green River and Rock Springs.

"Did you learn anything last night, Marshal?" Raven asked, riding alongside him, his hands no longer handcuffed, as Miles no longer considered him to be a threat or a murderer.

"I did. Enough to press for an investigation into the postmaster's death."

Reaching a natural rise in the land, Miles reined in.

Spread out before them were ramshackle buildings, the vast majority in disrepair, their false fronts collapsed. Sagebrush and weeds dotted the inhospitable landscape. Over to their left were the remnants of the railroad and a dilapidated water tower. Beyond a corral stocked with horses spread the cemetery.

"Welcome to my ghost town," Raven said.

Miles knew about the history of the area. The old settlement of Green River had been virtually abandoned when the Union Pacific moved the rail tracks west to Bryan, near the Black's Fork of the Green River. U.P. was only interested in building on land it owned, and didn't want to purchase the existing Green River plots. That was in the late 1860s. Then, in 1872 drought dried up the Black's Fork River. Since the trains needed an ample supply of water, U.P. transferred its site to Green River, Bryan's population moved with them and the town gradually died.

Raven pointed. "There's the corral and our home."

A black woman was hanging washing on a line. She spotted them approaching, a hand raised to shade her eyes. Then she grinned and waved at Raven.

"And that's my wife, Gwendolyn. At least she's grinning, so it can't be too bad."

"For someone who faces a hangman, you're mighty concerned about the reception you'll get from your wife!" Miles joked.

Raven ran a hand round his neck. "Don't remind me, Marshal."

Gwendolyn Raven cocked her head to one side as Miles and her husband dismounted just beyond the washing line. "Where've you been, Vincent? I've been awful worried."

"It's a long story, Gwen."

"And aren't you going to introduce your friend?"

"This is U.S. Marshal Miles." He hesitated then added, "I'm his prisoner. He's taking me to Cheyenne."

She dropped the basket and lifted her arms akimbo. "What?" Her eyes widened and she glared at Miles. "What's he supposed to have done, lawman?"

"He's been charged with murder—but I don't reckon he did it, Mrs. Raven."

She let out a big sigh. "Glad to hear it, Marshal Miles." She cast a concerned glance at her husband and then gestured to Miles. "You'd better come inside. Sit a spell while you tell me everything over a coffee."

"Obliged, ma'am," Miles said and gently nudged Raven ahead of him.

Raven needed no further urging and loped to his wife's side, interlacing his hand in hers. She peered up at him and from this angle Miles noticed moisture under her eye.

Their "home" was a single room in a dilapidated hut, holes in the roof plugged with boards. There were four straight-backed chairs and a table, an ancient stove and to one side, under the curtain that covered a window stood a brass bedstead.

Over a cup of java, Vincent told Gwendolyn his predicament.

Her hands clasped his. "And you didn't get a chance to wire our buyer?"

He barked a laugh. "Plain slipped my mind, Gwen!"

Letting go of him, she stood and folded her arms. "So, Marshal, what are you going to do about it? I sure don't want my man to hang."

"I'll recommend the trial be postponed while further investigations are made."

She sank back into her chair. "Your heart's in the right place, but I don't see how the real murderer can get caught now. Too much time has passed."

"I won't rest until I find the murderer, Mrs. Raven."

"But while you go looking, my husband's behind bars, not earning a crust."

"I can't help that," Miles said.

"No, I suppose not. We were banking on this latest sale …"

"You say the buyer's in Cheyenne?"

"Yes."

"Well, before I take Vincent to the prison, we can swing by to see your client."

Vincent whistled. "That's obligin' of you, Marshal."

Miles winked at Gwendolyn. "I wouldn't want to be responsible for your wife starving."

CHAPTER EIGHT

WILLIAM WILSON

Berenice had watched Cash ride to the north-west in the direction of the casino, and then swung on her heel and returned to her room. There was no more scratching behind her room's walls, she noticed with relief. If the critters were nocturnal, then she might have to spend another night with Cash. A warm feeling spread through her at the thought. No hardship at all, she thought as she slipped out of her dress.

Back in Boston, she would be regarded as a spinster left on the shelf at twenty-five, but she relished the freedom her single status gave her. While not promiscuous, she had already enjoyed several dalliances. She found Cash Laramie to be a considerate and pleasing lover. She'd passed her hands over his broad shoulders and rugged body with delight, but hadn't commented on the various scars or the arrowhead on a leather thong round his neck. They belonged to his past and were none of her business. His vibrant blue eyes had entranced her at their first meeting in Devon's office. In retrospect, last night's union had seemed inevitable, even if the mysterious scratching hadn't impelled her to seek an alternative sleeping arrangement. She had no illusions about him, for she believed he was a man destined to be alone, without commitment. She would revel in his company while she could, she decided.

Having changed into her riding skirt, blouse and jacket, and black lace-up boots, she descended the hotel stairs.

As she walked across the foyer she was waylaid by Mr. Allan.

"Miss Berenice, are you going out?" He stood in front of her, gaunt, almost predatory in black with a hooked nose, hands on lapels.

She was tempted to say she always dressed like this for lounging about on the veranda. "Yes, Mr. Allan. Do you have a problem with that?"

"No, of course not, Miss. I just like to keep cognizant of the whereabouts of our clientele—if anything unfortunate should occur ..."

"If you have a fire, be sure to check on my room, won't you?"

He took a step back and said in a haughty tone, "There's no need to be flippant, Miss Rohmer!"

She couldn't resist a smirk as in his umbrage he'd switched to her surname. "If you must know, I'm riding into town. I should return for lunch. Is that all right?"

He bowed ingratiatingly. "Take care, Miss. The trail is not too safe."

For a heart-churning instant she wondered if he'd given Horace a similar warning. "I will. Thank you for your concern."

She stepped onto the veranda and descended the steps. Her horse was saddled and ready; the stable-boy stood by the hitching rail. "Thank you, Jerry." His name was Jeremiah, but he preferred 'Jerry' she'd learned after a brief chat earlier. She gave him a smile and a tip. Then, politely declining his offer of help, she shoved her foot in the stirrup and swung into the saddle in one swift move.

The trail to town passed the undertaker's parlor, the large sign over the window stating, FUNERAL DIRECTOR. Good prices for coffins guaranteed. Prop. E. Price.

As she rode past, a tall slim man in his mid-forties came out. He had thinning black hair, a suitably pale complexion and a beaked nose. Seeing her, his thin lips approximated a smile that would hardly brighten a corpse. "Good morning, ma'am!"

A thought struck her and she reined in next to the boardwalk that fronted the funeral parlor. "Good morning, sir."

"I'm Elisha Price, the town undertaker. Pleased to meet you."

"Not too pleased, I trust," she suggested.

His dark brown eyes danced in confusion. "Pardon?"

"I don't wish to be one of your clients, sir," she elaborated with a faint smile.

"Oh, yes, I see!" He wasn't among the walking dead after all, for his complexion colored slightly around the gills. "I'm afraid I do have that effect on people."

She leaned forward, confidingly. He took a pace closer. "Do you know my brother, Horace Rohmer? He was a guest at the hotel."

He pursed his lips, stroked his prominent chin and glanced down, evading her eyes. "Rohmer ..." Finally, he shook his head and leveled his gaze at her in a steady stare. "No, I'm sorry, I have not encountered the name before. Why do you ask?"

She straightened in the saddle. "He's gone missing."

"Oh, I'm distressed to hear that," he said, though his features reflected no emotion whatsoever. Perhaps she was being uncharitable; weren't undertakers supposed to show no emotion? "I hope you locate him soon."

"Thank you, Mr. Price. I dearly hope so too." She eased her horse away from the boardwalk and at her gentle urging the horse broke into a canter. She long ago learned that someone who vowed something while offering a steady stare was invariably lying. She wondered why the undertaker would lie about knowing Horace.

The trail leading to Rock Springs proved quite safe and uneventful and she wondered if Mr. Allan would be disappointed to learn that.

The bank was in the middle of the main street. She halted her chestnut at the rail and dismounted. Out of the corner of her eye she noticed that a handful of men strolling past gave her a cursory look but kept on walking. A woman astride a horse was not unusual here in the west, she knew; back east, her mode of riding would have evinced opprobrium if not outright censure.

She secured the horse and strode through the bank's door. There was a small queue of two men and a woman. She joined them and bided her time as they slowly shuffled forward to the single counter with a grille. Eventually, she was faced with the teller, who said, "How may I help you, ma'am?"

It was not the first time she'd been addressed as such. She supposed as she was twenty-five, she should be wed by now. "I wish to speak to your manager. It is most urgent."

"Oh, you should have said earlier, ma'am. There was no need to join the queue."

"So I can see him now?"

"Yes, ma'am. And your name is?"

She told him and her heart gave a little lift as she noted recognition in the teller's eyes. So Horace had been in here!

Shortly, she was led past a folding counter top and into an office at the rear on the right. The door stated: William Wilson, Bank Manager.

The teller knocked on the door and opened it. "Miss Berenice Rohmer to see you, Mr. Wilson."

Wilson was portly, ruddy-faced, with gimlet eyes, a shock of unruly grey hair, and a lopsided mouth. He stood as she entered. "Take a seat, Miss Rohmer," he slurred. She noticed that his vest was blemished with dark red stains. She hastily scanned the room and

61

spotted a half full carafe of red wine and four crystal glasses on a sideboard to the right.

"Thank you, Mr. Wilson. It is good of you to see me at such short notice."

"Would you like a drink?" His gaze moved from her to a small round mirror on his desk. He licked his lips.

She smiled sweetly. "No, it is a little early for me, thank you." She refrained from saying *Go ahead, don't mind me.*

She observed a battle of will-power in his features, his grey eyes darting to the ceiling, to the carafe and then to her. Finally, he gave a shudder, leaned forward on his elbows and after two abortive attempts managed to steeple his fingers. "Mr. Rohmer must be your brother, since you introduced yourself as 'Miss,' is that not so?"

"That is correct, Mr. Wilson. Can you confirm that Horace withdrew the money wired to him?"

Wilson looked sideways at the small mirror. He arched his eyebrows, murmured something unintelligible to the reflection, and then turned his attention to her. "Yes, and he was charming. A real gentleman."

"Did he seem worried, concerned in any way?"

He screwed-up his eyes and studied the mirror again. "Did he?" he whispered to the reflection. After a brief pause, he said, "No, not particularly. It was a great deal of cash to carry, however." He shifted in his seat and one of his elbows slipped off the desk surface and he hastily righted himself, sitting back in the chair, offering an inane smile.

She recalled what Cash had said and decided to extrapolate on that. "Was anybody with my brother when he made the withdrawal?"

Wilson raised a hand, the fingers shaking slightly, as if attempting to waylay a memory. He eyed the carafe, the mirror, and then sighed. "I *do* remember him. It was Mr. Corman, he was at his side, shoulder to shoulder you might say."

"Who is Mr. Corman?"

"Usher Corman is a ... a ..." He glared at the mirror, raised an eyebrow. "... a freelance. Presently, he works for the lawyer Rufus Wilmot. I can assure you, your brother was in safe hands with Mr. Corman by his side. He's very good at what he does."

"And what is that, Mr. Wilson?"

His tongue flicked over his lips. "Corman is reputed to be a hired gunman."

That seemed hopeful, she thought. Horace had probably been provided with the Corman fellow as an escort or bodyguard since he was taking out so much money. The baron would be prudent where large sums of money were concerned, she supposed. And it made sense for him to employ a local lawyer to transact business.

One dark cloud persisted, however: she still couldn't square why Horace hadn't telegraphed her. That was another line of inquiry, however.

She stood. "Thank you for your time, sir. You have been most helpful."

Shakily Mr. Wilson got to his feet. "Pleasure to be of assistance, ma'am, er Miss ..." He scuttled round his desk, faltered, supported himself with a hand on a chair back, and then reached the door and opened it for her.

"Good day, sir."

"Ma... er, Miss." Before he closed the door, she noticed him eyeing the carafe.

Next stop was the telegraph office, which was also on the main street.

But the telegraphist was of little help. "No, Mr. Rohmer hasn't been in. I'd seen him about, as I take note of influential strangers in our town. He was a real gent, by all accounts."

* * *

Miles gave the Ravens a few minutes alone in their shack to say their goodbyes while he brought a bucket of water for the horses. They'd had success digging a well, it seemed, though they said it was barely enough water for sustenance, and not sufficient for farmland irrigation.

They set off with Mrs. Raven's words ringing in their ears: "Come along home to Jesus, come along home to me, Vince!"

After about an hour, still riding into the sun, the ground now undulated ahead of them, dotted with boulders, upthrust rocks, bushes and stunted trees. Birds chirped. All was peaceful.

The first bullet knocked Miles's hat into the air, the second creased his forehead as he jumped off his horse. A rifle's report echoed, shattering the peace.

Two more shots were fired in quick succession. Another rifle or the same one?

Hampered by his handcuffs, Raven was slower in dismounting and let out a growl as his boots hit dirt.

Colt cocked in his hand, Miles hid behind his mount's rump, holding the reins tight to control the animal. He squinted in the glare, scanning the horizon left, right and ahead. Over on the left was a rocky knoll; he reckoned the ambusher was hiding there. "You hurt?" he called to Raven, who was also using his horse as a shield.

"Yeah, but it's only a shoulder wound. I can shoot if you want me to."

Miles tossed over the keys to the handcuffs and Raven deftly caught them. His horse shied but he restrained it. Miles then stretched up and unsheathed his Winchester from its boot. "Here," he said, and threw Raven his Colt.

His hands free now, Raven caught the six-gun with ease. "I don't reckon a handgun can reach their hideout." He gestured vaguely in the direction of the knoll crowned by several rugged rocks.

Miles replied, "I doubt if you could use the rifle with a wounded shoulder."

"Fair enough. If anyone gets near enough, I'll be sure to plug him."

Two rifle shots sounded and Raven's horse whinnied and buckled at the legs, falling sideways, almost crushing Raven.

The horse cried in agony. Raven used the Colt to put it out of its misery. "Swines!" the horse-trader barked and swore, instantly diving behind the carcase.

"I reckon they don't want you to catch the train!" Miles shouted.

Two more shots echoed and Miles's horse was hit. Miles backed off in time and then dropped behind the animal's body. "We're pinned down here!"

CHAPTER NINE

THE OVAL PORTRAIT

Berenice urged the chestnut on, pushing the poor brute hard. She didn't know why she was in a hurry. Cash wouldn't return from the baron's casino for hours yet. She dearly wanted to fall into his arms and be consoled.

Curse you, Horace, what have you gotten into? Throughout their childhood, she'd been the reckless one, always getting into scrapes, whether that was falling into the stream, climbing trees or raiding neighboring orchards. Horace was the sensible one, the pacifier. But this latest venture appeared not only hair-brained but also mortally serious. She truly feared for Horace's life.

The sun was high and hot and she was glad of the hat. Sweat soaked the back of her blouse and armpits. She wiped her face with a gloved hand.

She was riding along a gully when she heard the shots. A rifle—no, two—spaced out. Slowly, she eased on the reins, pulled the chestnut to a halt. Mr. Allan's warning about the trail not being safe sent her thoughts scurrying. She dismounted. Her mouth was dry but it wasn't from the trail dust.

Leaving the reins under a big rock, she withdrew the Winchester and ratcheted a slug into the barrel. Slipping her hat back on its drawstring, she felt the heat of the sun on her brow. Treading carefully, she clambered up the scree of the gully, her boots soon covered in dust.

As she reached the lip of the gully, she immediately sank down.

In those few seconds she'd taken in the alarming scene.

Two black men were being fired upon by a blond bearded man. It seemed obvious that the blond shooter had ambushed the pair, since both of their horses appeared to be dead.

For a fleeting instant she spotted the glint of metal on the nearest black man, the one with a rifle. A lawman's badge, a sheriff or marshal, probably. Then the blond was a criminal.

Steeling herself, she raised the Winchester to her shoulder and took aim.

She let off three shots in quick succession, ignoring the kick of the stock against her shoulder. Her bullets kicked up dust and shards of stone close to the blond man's head. He jerked back, slid behind a boulder. She fired two more shots at the boulder.

And then she heard a horse whinny and its hoofs pound, the sound diminishing. She reckoned that he'd skedaddled.

Wiping a sleeve over her brow, she lifted her rifle and waved at the pair hiding behind their horses.

They waved back, all grins, and stood up.

* * *

It was past mid-day when Cash spotted a rider approaching him from the rear. He shifted in the saddle and flipped the thong off the hammer of his Colt, just in case, and then slowed his horse to a trot.

"Hello, there!" the rider called, slowing to ride alongside. He was blond with a beard and moustache, his long hair falling to his shoulders. He lifted his grey Stetson, wiped the leather inner band with a checked shirt sleeve. "You headed for the Lenore Casino?"

"Yes. I have business with the owner." He showed the badge. "Marshal Laramie."

"Usher Corman." He leaned over and they shook hands. "I work at the Lenore Casino spread. I'll accompany you there, if that's all right?"

"Sure," Cash said, though he wondered if "accompany" was the right word. He felt as if he was under an armed escort. For the rest of the journey Cash diverted all questions about the reason for his visit, and attempted to learn more about the casino and the baron.

"The baron's one of those eccentric Europeans," Corman explained. "He's a good employer, and generous as well, even if he's very strict."

"I heard he named the casino after his late wife," Cash prompted.

"Yeah. That was tragic. Before her death, it was going to be named The Corinthian Casino."

"She died out here, then?"

"Yeah. She'd gone at night—nobody knows why... The baron reckons she was sleep-walking. They found her body next day. She wasn't a pretty sight; she'd been savaged by wolves, her heart ripped out and eaten."

"That must have been terrible for him."

"It changed the man. That same day the baron got his brace of shotguns and went alone hunting for the wolves. Two days later, he came back wild-eyed with the pelts of three of the critters."

* * *

Long before they reached the entrance to the casino complex, Cash and Corman rode past dozens of white-painted wooden posts, all lined up neatly: "Setting out the lots for the baron's town plan," Corman explained.

Finally, an entrance arch of Doric columns declared "The Lenore Casino." From here curved a wide drive bordered with sagebrush flowering yellow, red, pink and orange; mixed with these were sego lily and larkspur. The drive led to a long two-storey building, its veranda graced with a series of Corinthian columns. A rooftop terrace commanded a view of the surrounding countryside, and above the entrance doors, rising from the center, was a latticework tower with a huge clock-face showing Roman numerals; a big metal pendulum swung below, partly visible through a long narrow window above the entrance.

They tethered the horses at a hitching rail at the front steps.

A good distance away on their right was a marble edifice, with a life-size winged angel on top.

"That's the baron's little mausoleum," Corman explained, his voice thick and laced with gravel. "It's where his wife's buried—minus her heart."

Then without saying more he led Cash up the steps and through the double doors. To one side was a Chinese sentry dressed in black and gold livery, brass buttons to his throat. He carried a sword at his belt but made no move to challenge Cash, recognizing Corman.

They entered an atrium clad in dark oak panels, the floor tiled with patterned marble. A double staircase swept to a landing with a series of double doors. "Up there," Corman pointed, "is a ballroom, a concert hall and a couple of dining rooms, a salon for the ladies and the baron's private rooms." The landing was almost on a level with the clock's metronomic pendulum.

Smartly dressed men and women strolled through the atrium, arm in arm, none of them taking any notice of Cash and Corman's trail-dusted attire. Several Chinese in black and gold costumes moved to and fro, carrying newspapers, documents, and silver trays of drinks and cakes.

Cash peered up and could distinctly hear the pendulum as it scythed through air.

He lowered his gaze and spotted a man striding purposefully toward them.

"Meet the baron," Corman said, removing his hat.

Baron von Kempelen was virtually the same height as Cash. He wore a monocle in his left eye, possessed a scar down his left cheek, and sported a Van Dyke moustache, which was as blond as his short-cropped hair. He wore a grey suit of cavalry twill, with waistcoat, and shining black shoes. Cash noted a slight bulge in the vest pocket; doubtless a derringer snug in there.

"Corman, who is this with you?" the baron asked curtly.

"Baron, sir, this here is U.S. Marshal Laramie."

Appraising his clothes, the baron said, "You are not here for leisure, Marshal."

Cash took off his hat. "No, Baron. I'm here in an official capacity." He glanced around. "Can we talk in private?"

Von Kempelen's unencumbered grey-green eye danced erratically then settled again on Cash. "You have me intrigued." With one hand he made a shooing gesture to Corman. "Thank you, you can go now."

Wiping a hand over his bristly chin, Corman nodded. "Sure, Baron. I need to clean up." He put on his hat, swung on his heel and went out the entrance doorway.

"I noticed your interest in my clock," the baron said, gazing at the swinging pendulum.

"Yeah, it's unusual. I reckon I can feel the breeze it makes as it swings."

"I had it specially made for me by a family acquaintance, Sigmund Riefler. The firm of Clemens Riefler is situated in Munich, my home city and it is known for its precision pendulum clocks."

"I'm impressed, Baron."

"German engineering is the best in the world, Marshal. Now, my office is not far. We will talk there."

"Fine by me, Baron. Lead on."

He was led to the right, through a double door that was guarded by a huge Chinese man in a smart black and gold suit and a sword with belt. They trod on thick carpets that went through three gaming rooms where patrons played on a variety of roulette wheels or card tables. Chinese male and female staff darted between people, serving trays of liquor. A smoke mist hovered above their heads; the ceiling, where visible, appeared stained.

"Quite an enterprise you have here, Baron."

Von Kempelen chuckled. "It is my honey to attract the flies." He didn't elaborate and pushed open a door into a large office.

Hanging over a huge broad desk was a large oval portrait of a dark-haired, sultry woman with skin the color of porcelain and eyes that seemed inscrutable. Cash had seen smaller similar portraits at a distance hanging in every room they passed through. "A striking lady," he observed.

"Yes. My late wife, Lenore."

"Sorry for your loss, Baron."

"Thank you."

A Chinese sentry stepped in behind them and closed the door.

"Take a seat, Marshal," the baron said, lowering himself into the chair behind his desk.

As Cash settled into a leather armchair opposite him, the baron said, "Whiskey?"

"No, thanks. Water would be fine."

The baron clicked his fingers and grunted, "Wang." The sentry called Wang bowed and moved to the collection of drinks on the ornate table to one side. The man clearly understood English and poured a tumbler of amber liquid and then emptied half a carafe of water into another glass.

"I see most of your staff is Chinese," Cash said.

"Yes. Those who I employ speak good English and they know their place."

"Their place, Baron?"

"They're a subservient race. Masters at kowtowing, you know. They accept the superiority of Germans and serve well." He wafted a hand at Cash. "Tell me, what is your official business, Marshal?" Wang handed him his drink, face impassive.

Cash was given his water, and then Wang bowed and moved to the door, where he continued to stand sentinel. "I'm attempting to locate a businessman, Horace Rohmer."

"Ah, yes, I know of him." He sipped his whiskey. "I was expecting him, since he was interested in buying a good number of lots. One of the flies, you see?"

"Ah, yes, now I understand."

Von Kempelen shook his head. "But Mr. Rohmer never showed up."

"He definitely came here, Baron. The hotel has a record of his visit, and the livery man still has a horse on loan to Mr. Rohmer."

"That is a puzzle, then. I thought he'd had thought, no, how you say, second thoughts. But now you say he came here?"

Cash nodded, swallowing the water, his eyes not leaving the baron's.

Finishing the whiskey in one gulp, the baron wiped his mouth with the back of his hand. "I hope he wasn't waylaid and robbed ..."

"That must now be a real consideration for us."

The baron's free eye did that merry dance again then pierced Cash. "Us?"

"I traveled with his sister. Naturally, she's anxious to locate him. Particularly as he was carrying a great deal of money."

"That must be most distressful for her, no?"

"You could say that, Baron."

Von Kempelen stood, adjusted his jacket. "What more can I say, Marshal? It looks as if you have made a wasteful journey."

Did he believe the baron?

CHAPTER TEN

"CONTRIBUTORS"

Her heart pounding, Berenice rode down to the ambushed men. Amidst a flurry of dust she hastily dismounted.

"Thanks for coming to our rescue, ma'am," said the lawman.

"It's Miss Rohmer," she corrected.

He gestured with his hat that had a hole in it. "U.S. Marshal Miles." He turned to his companion. "This here's Mr. Raven. Did you get a good look at the varmint who bushwhacked us?"

"I didn't see his face. He was blond, his hair was long, he had a beard and he wore Levi's, a checked shirt and a grey Stetson."

"That's a good description." Miles shook his head. "But it doesn't tally with anyone I've met."

"Are you both all right?" she asked.

"I was hit in the shoulder," said Raven. "I'll live—till the hangman, leastways."

She eyed Miles. "Mr. Raven's your prisoner?"

"For the moment, Miss. He's quite harmless."

She raised a hand to his forehead. "You're bleeding, Marshal."

"Only a scratch, Miss Rohmer." He pointed at her Winchester. "Fancy shooting, if I may say so."

"You're the second U.S. Marshal hereabouts to compliment me on my gun work."

"Another? I wonder if know him …"

"You do. He's Cash Laramie. Your boss sent him to accompany me."

"Now that *is* interesting! He sure gets all the tough assignments!"

She looked askance at him then her cheeks dimpled as he chuckled.

Then the cast of his features became serious as he peered at the dead horses.

"What are you going to do?" she asked.

"If I might impose, Miss Rohmer, I'd appreciate it if you'd ride back to Rock Springs; bring the sheriff, the doctor and two horses."

"Yes, of course, Marshal," she answered.

Berenice didn't spare the chestnut on her ride to town.

Breathlessly, she first tackled the sheriff. Fortunately, at mention of U.S. Marshal Miles, the lawman was spurred into action.

Within a short while, almost before she could catch her breath, she was riding out with the sheriff, the doctor and two horses in tow.

Marshal Miles was effusive in his thanks, but she brushed his words aside. "I'm only too pleased to help, Marshal. What will you do now?"

"I'll go after the bushwhacker. The sheriff here can take Mr. Raven into town where the doc can treat that wound."

"What about you?" she asked in concern.

He dabbed it with a hand; it was dry. "A scratch. I've had worse, Miss Rohmer."

She gestured at her chestnut. "I think he's rested some. I'd best return to the hotel. Marshal, if you resolve the matter with your ambusher, perhaps you could swing by to see your friend, Cash?"

"I might do that, Miss. Safe journey."

* * *

After the doctor and the sheriff had left with Raven, Miles rode his fresh mount to the rocky knoll that had concealed the ambusher.

There were traces. He dismounted and studied the tracks.

He detected a distinctive heel mark from the left boot, like a sickle shape, and the right fore-hoof of the horse revealed a small double-oh indentation where two stones must have damaged the horseshoe.

Enough to go on, he reckoned, swinging into the saddle.

* * *

Letting the chestnut find his pace, Berenice headed back to the hotel. A gnawing sensation squatted in her gut. She wasn't prone to worry or foreboding, but something was troubling her. Maybe it was reaction to the recent excitement? She'd never shot at a person before; that had to be unsettling. And she wondered about that prisoner, Raven; what had he done? The sheriff from Rock Springs was amenable enough and didn't insist on handcuffs. Of course the poor fellow was wounded. The doctor had bandaged Mr. Raven, saying that he'd remove the bullet in his surgery when they got back.

Yes, maybe that was why her nerves were all a-jangle.

When she rode up to the livery stable at the rear of the hotel, she was met by Jerry. At sight of him her troubles seemed to fall away. His face lit up. She dismounted and handed him the reins of the chestnut. "I'll give him a good grooming, Miss Rohmer!" Jerry promised.

"Thank you. I appreciate it. He's been a busy critter today!"

Jerry's brow creased but she didn't bother to explain.

She used her gloves to brush trail dust from her riding skirt and blouse. "I need a drink!"

The foyer and reception desk were vacant.

She peered in the dining room. Nobody there. It was too early, probably. She looked in the lounge next door and spotted the drinks trolley.

But there was no bottle of that rather pleasant amontillado.

Her mouth curved in a smile of devilment. Neither Madeline nor Roderick were about, and no staff either.

She recalled which direction he'd gone to get the bottle last night and soon found the door leading to the cellar.

* * *

Bathed in the cellar's flickering lantern light, Willard Frey sat in his underwear, his hands tied behind the chair back. His cheeks and chin were bloody and his eyes were closed. His chin rested on his slowly rising blood-spattered chest.

Roderick glared at the salesman and swiveled round to face Wilmot. "What's the matter now? Can't you see I'm busy? This fool's hidden his money somewhere, but he won't tell me where!"

"Then he's no fool, is he?" suggested Wilmot, his grey eyes shining in the light.

"He must have spent a small fortune on those machines."

"Well, why not get rid of him and install the slot-machines in the hotel? They might bring in a surprising amount."

"It has crossed my mind. I'd have to get Maddy to fake a bill of sale, I suppose."

"I thought that was my province."

"Yes, of course, Rufus. It's been a while since you've performed that service for us."

"Well, right now I'm thinking maybe I should stop performing any service for you both."

"Oh, why is that?" The question grated, the tone deepening.

"I know Maddy's the one with the imagination, Roddy. But try using yours. I know for sure there are two U.S. Marshals in the area. They must be onto us!"

* * *

Berenice descended the cellar steps and licked her lips, anticipating a glass or two of the wine.

She heard muffled voices as the stairs curved round.

Perhaps she should go back?

No, why should she? She was a client, and wanted a glass of amontillado. She'd simply ask for one and doubtless embarrass the staff into the bargain!

She reached the bottom step and stopped abruptly. Roderick stood talking to a white-haired man. Their facial expressions were not happy. And then she let out an involuntary gasp as she saw Mr. Frey in the chair behind them. Her heart somersaulted and she swung round, riding skirt flaring.

"Wait!" Roderick called to her.

She didn't wait. She'd seen the blood on Mr. Frey's face and chest.

Seconds later, something hard slammed into her back, forced her onto the steps and winded her. Her knees banged against the riser and she yelped.

"Get off me!" she screamed as a hand wrenched her left arm up her back. A heavy weight pressed on her back, crushing the air from her as she felt the stairs digging into her chest.

"Stand up and come quietly," Roderick said gruffly. "Or I'll break your arm!"

"All right," she wheezed.

Slowly, she was let up. Her shins, thighs and chest must be bruised, she thought.

Shakily, she staggered down into the cellar.

"Who's this?"

"Miss Berenice Rohmer," Roderick said.

"*Rohmer!*" the man exclaimed.

"Calm down, Rufus. We'll deal with her. You have no need to worry yourself."

"I've had enough, Roddy. I'm getting my money and leaving town. You should do the same!"

"But Rufus, we've got a good thing going here!"

"Not anymore!"

The man stormed toward the stairs.

"What are we going to do with you, hmm?" queried Roderick. As if in answer, he looped a length of rope round her hands and tied them tightly behind her back.

* * *

Cash returned from the casino complex, intent on asking the funeral director about the body of the baron's wife. He'd never heard of wolves eating an entire heart. The story didn't square, somehow. Though he had to confess it was second-hand; from Corman, not the baron. He rode past the cemetery. To his right was a freshly dug open grave, but no grave-digger in evidence. Halting his horse outside the funeral parlor, he secured the reins at the post and climbed the entrance steps, using his hat to pat away trail dust from his sleeves. He was about to knock on the glass front door and enter when he heard a scuffling sound and gasping.

Unmistakeable. Someone in the throes of lovemaking, he reckoned.

"Oh, Elisha, hurry!" breathed Madeline Allan.

Elisha groaned, grunted and gasped.

Feeling like a voyeur, Cash backed away.

"Yesss!" Madeline hissed.

They're two adults, he told himself. It was no business of his what they got up to; he reckoned they could have chosen a more private venue to indulge themselves. Fleetingly, the carnal interlude excited a recollection of his night with Berenice. Shaking off that warm memory, he decided to approach Elisha Price later.

As he descended the steps, he noticed a black lace ribbon snagged on a protruding nail. He plucked it free and pocketed it.

Untying his horse, he led it to the stables and went inside, the cool semi-darkness a welcome and complete contrast to the heat of the day.

The first thing he noticed was Frey's buckboard. Still loaded and ready to go, though no horse in the traces yet.

Young Jeremiah emerged from a stall, a grooming brush in his hand. "Howdy, Marshal."

"Hello, Jerry. I see Mr. Frey hasn't left yet. He's leaving it mighty late for the ride, isn't he?"

"I don't know about that, sir. Mr. Allan did tell me that Mr. Frey wasn't too well. Unfit to travel today, he said ..."

"That's a shame. He was looking forward to selling his machines."

"I hope I'm not talking out of turn, Marshal, but I reckon Mr. Frey's all bluster. He couldn't sell no straw to me the way he talks."

"It's just his way, Jerry. You concentrate on the product, not the salesman. If you want it, it doesn't matter how the salesman comes across, you'll buy it."

"Well, I sure wouldn't buy nothin' from him."

"The impetuosity of youth!" Cash laughed. "I was the same at one time. Stand by your ideals while you can, son."

"Miss Berenice is different. Now, she could sell me anything at all …"

"Yeah, she is, isn't she?"

"I've not seen much of her, Marshal, but already I'm mighty fond of her."

Cash grinned. "I know, she has that way about her. Direct, but not rude."

"Straight, I call it, Marshal."

Cash rubbed a hand over Jerry's hair. "When you're older, you'll appreciate her even more, I'm sure."

"When I'm older, sir? I'll have you know I'm fifteen next month!"

"Yep. Old enough. I'm going to see her now, so I'll be sure to tell her you've been asking after her."

Jerry's face flushed. "You will?"

"Sure."

He left Jerry gawping and made his way to the front of the hotel.

The reception desk was unattended, and there was no staff in evidence. He wondered how they made the place pay.

He ascended the stairs and took his time to walk along the corridor to her door. He wondered what kind of mood she'd be in.

She hadn't been too happy about him leaving her behind.

And she wasn't going to be pleased with his negative report from the baron.

He knocked on her door, but there was no answer. He tried the handle. Locked. He called her name, not too loud, in case there were any guests dozing. No response.

Retracing his steps, he went down to the reception desk. And it still wasn't manned. Hadn't Madeline returned from the funeral parlor yet? Maybe they'd indulged in a second session; if so, he admired the undertaker's stamina.

That thought generated another, a memory of last night. An experience he'd like to repeat tonight, perhaps. If she was in the mood.

Then he sensed a sinking feeling in his stomach. Had Berenice left the hotel? Surely not.

He checked the register. No, probably not; she hadn't signed out, anyway. Though that didn't mean anything, he supposed. If she'd left in anger …

His heart overturned. What if she'd set off for the casino and their paths hadn't crossed?

Cash rushed out and went back to the stables.

* * *

Madeline descended the cellar steps and paused at the bottom, seeing Berenice sitting in a chair next to Frey; she was gagged and tied hand and foot. Madeline darted a look at Roderick. "What are you doing?"

"She came down, I had no choice," he said.

Madeline's mismatched eyes darkened, her face stern. Bending slightly so she was face-to-face with Berenice, she said, "You want to be with your brother?"

Berenice stared wide-eyed, struggling against her bonds.

"I'll take that as a 'yes.' It can be arranged." She turned to Roderick. "Bring her up!"

"What about Frey?" he asked.

"Is he still alive?"

He lifted Frey's eyelid. "Yes, though barely."

"After we've dealt with her, we'll put him in one of his crates, take the buckboard."

"We can't be leaving?" he whined. "After all we've invested and done!"

Her lips curled in distaste. "No, you fool, we're not going anywhere. We'll ride out and dump Frey and the buckboard down Clegg gorge. It'll look like an accident. He was on his way to the casino and got lost."

"Yes. That could work."

"It *will* work! Now, bring her up."

Roderick struggled to drag Berenice upstairs. He wasn't nearly as strong as Elisha, Madeline mused. Finally, they reached Berenice's room. The black cat

Pluto followed them. Madeline unlocked and opened the door.

Roderick flung Berenice onto the bedstead and tied her hands to the brass posts of the headboard.

Madeline said, "Let's get decorating!"

Obediently, Roderick rushed out, opened a service cupboard on the opposite side of the corridor and took rolls of flock wallpaper, a bucket of paste mix, a brush and a knife.

Berenice stared in shock as they used the knife to cut through the flock wallpaper to reveal a section of preformed wood-panel wall.

Roderick used a hammer to pry out the nails and the section of wall came away in one piece. She'd heard of prefabricated homes, but this was the first example she'd seen.

Madeline adjusted the curtain and let in more light from the window.

Berenice gasped, involuntarily sucking in the gag, which almost choked her. Frantically breathing through her nose, she stared.

Behind the left-hand section of wall, within the narrow cavity, stood the slumped form of Horace, tethered to wooden slats that served as a frame for the partition wall. His fingers were raw, his stare opaque, his mouth stretched by a tight cloth gag.

Flies buzzed.

Her stomach roiled and she feared that she'd vomit and choke.

With an effort, she swallowed bile and sickly stomach contents. Her head swam.

Madeline snarled, "Get her in there, Roddy."

She thrashed against them but they the pair were too strong for her. And she was weak with shock and remorse. Horace had been scratching at the wall and she and Cash had thought it was rats!

And now it was to be her fate too.

"It would be so easy to dump you in the cemetery, my dear," said Madeline, "but our little business has such a big turnover we'd overfill the place and people would soon get suspicious. This way, we have plenty of wall-space. We might have to order an extension from the catalogue."

"When we first started, we buried our contributor in the country," Roderick added conversationally, "but the wolves soon dug him up. Voracious devils, those wolves. That was awkward, but it was explained away, the poor fellow walked in his sleep and got lost ... Terrible what happened to the baron's wife."

"So, putting our contributors in the wall cavities serves us best," Madeline said.

Roderick screwed-up his eyes. "You look puzzled. Ah, 'contributors,' is that it."

Feebly, Berenice nodded.

"Our term for travelers with money, lots of money, my dear." He shoved her against the wood slats, tied one of her wrists to it. "They contribute to our nest-egg."

Somewhere a cat purred. Or was it Madeline?

CHAPTER ELEVEN

COFFIN FOR CASH

Cash entered the stable and was surprised to see that Berenice's chestnut was still there. Jerry was grooming Cash's horse.

"Hey, Jerry, any idea where Miss Rohmer could be?"

Jerry thumbed at the chestnut. "She went out earlier, Marshal, but she came in a while ago. I'd rubbed him down as he was in quite a lather." Her saddle and equipment rested on top of a stall wall.

Instinct or a sixth sense prompted Cash to withdraw her Winchester.

It was faint, but a definite powder smell; the rifle had been fired recently. He replaced the gun in its scabbard. She'd been trying her hand, no doubt, proving to herself that she was a better shot than her brother.

No point in hanging around here. He'd return to the hotel. Maybe Madeline was back from wherever she'd got to.

Once in the foyer, Cash saw that the reception desk was vacant. Then he spotted movement over toward the guest lounge next to the dining room.

He strode to the doorway and entered.

Standing by the drinks counter was Elisha Price; he was being served by Madeline.

She noted his entry. "Would you like a drink, Marshal?" she asked. "Dinner will be late, I'm afraid; the kitchen staff won't be here for another hour or so."

"Thanks. A beer."

"Coming up, sir!" she said, smiling.

He noticed the drinks trolley to one side, stocked no doubt for the dining room later. No amontillado in evidence, though. "Have you seen Miss Rohmer?" he asked.

She cocked her head while pouring from a bottle into his glass. "I imagine she's in her room."

He shrugged. "I'll try later. I understand she'd been riding. Maybe she went to lie down."

"That's probably it."

"I noticed Mr. Frey's slot machines are still loaded in the stables. How is he?"

"Oh, it's most unfortunate; he took ill sudden and had to cancel his visit to the baron. He's been confined to bed, poor man."

Roderick entered, rolling down his shirt sleeves, carrying his jacket over an arm. "Why, hi there, Marshal. I see you're being taken care of all right."

"Yes, thanks." He turned to Madeline and withdrew from his pocket the black lace ribbon he'd found. "Is it yours?"

Her eyes lit up. "Yes, it is. Where'd you find it?"

"On the doorstep of the funeral parlor ..."

Her cheeks flushed and her eyes darkened. She snatched it off him, shoved it under the counter.

"What were you doing at the funeral parlor, dearest?" Roderick asked, his tone deepening.

Cash was surprised to see guilt in her eyes. He noticed that Roderick was staring at Elisha now. What was the problem?

"You love *me*!" Roderick snapped, his voice rising, his eyes watering. "No one else!"

Realization dawned and Cash thought, not healthy, and moved away from the counter.

Unexpectedly, Roderick pounced on Elisha, his hands round the undertaker's neck. Elisha's back thudded into the counter.

"Stop it!" Madeline screamed.

"I've suspected for a while!" Roderick grated between clenched teeth.

Elisha tried clawing at his attacker's hands. Even though by all appearances he was the stronger man, he wasn't able to budge the manic grip and his complexion paled as the blood-flow was stifled.

This had gone on far enough, Cash thought. He took a pace toward them and was deafened by two quick explosions near his face.

His world went black.

* * *

Madeline held the smoking pistol, her hand shaking. She'd taken life before, but this was very different. Tears blurred her vision.

Her twin brother Roderick's body lay on the floor, a bloody bullet hole in his shirt discoloring the chest area. She shuddered, seeing him staring open mouthed. She'd loved him and enjoyed his body, but she loved Elisha more.

Wiping away tears with her free hand, she took in the supine form of the marshal, a red gash on his temple, blood oozing into his eye and down the side of his face.

She dropped the gun on the counter. "It's all going wrong!"

Elisha rested a hand on hers. "We have to get rid of the bodies!"

She ran her hands over her face and let out a moan. "Another wall cavity?"

"No … the coffins."

"I thought you couldn't risk using too many?"

"That was before. We've got to get away now. Roderick's absence will have to be explained, then there's the marshal … with another one in the area. We have no choice, my love, we must make a run for it!"

My love. That endearment gave her strength. "I'm sorry, Elisha. But he was throttling you!"

He squeezed her hands. "I know. He would've killed me. He must have gone over the edge, otherwise he wouldn't have attacked me in front of the marshal."

She scanned the room, gestured at the two bodies. "How can we move them?"

"The drinks trolley. One at a time!"

She eyed the wall clock. "We've got an hour before the kitchen staff arrives."

"Let's get moving, then!" He pushed the trolley to the counter. Between them, they emptied it of all the bottles, placing them on the counter top.

Elisha was slim and wiry, but deceptively strong. She'd often felt those taut muscles, hard and powerful as he embraced her in stolen moments. "Developed over years of hauling corpses around, my dear," he'd said once in a romantic interlude.

Now, Elisha lifted the marshal with ease onto his shoulder and then lowered the body to the trolley. Its wheels squealed slightly in protest as he pushed it to the door of the lounge. "Check the way's clear!" he told her.

Casting a glance at her brother's body, she lifted her skirts and ran to the door, entered the foyer. Nobody about, as she'd expected.

"Hurry! It's all clear!"

"Grab a blanket from the cupboard," he instructed as he wheeled the trolley across the foyer floor.

She raced to the reception counter, went behind it and opened a cupboard, extracted an Indian-style blanket. Hurrying to his side, she draped it over the marshal.

Once outside the hotel entrance, Elisha wheeled the trolley along the boardwalk to the far corner. She helped him negotiate the end steps and then it became more difficult for the wheels to cross the uneven and rutted ground between the hotel and the funeral parlor.

She kept glancing at the corral and stables area over her left shoulder. The revolver was on the lounge bar counter. If young Jeremiah caught them, she didn't know what she'd do. Killing innocent people was not a problem, but they were slain for their money; Jeremiah was a mere child, and almost penniless.

They hauled the trolley up the steps. Elisha opened the double doors and they rushed inside. She breathed easier then.

"We can't do that again," Elisha said. "I'll take the carriage round. The horses are already in their traces since I was due to pick up Mrs. McGill's body later today."

He pushed the trolley through the building to the rear and onto the raised loading bay. He hurried to the gleaming black hearse carriage, its sides being two oval glass windows, and then drove it to the bay area, the decorative black tassels jiggling. He dumped the blanket in the rear of the hearse and then between them they manhandled the marshal into the coffin already secured there by two spikes jutting out of the floor.

At his instruction, they carried another coffin and slid it on top of that occupied by Marshal Laramie.

Working as fast as they could, she closed the rear doors and they climbed to the front seat. He drove the carriage to the entrance of the hotel.

Jumping down to the veranda, Elisha hurried through the foyer into the lounge. Her brother lay where he'd fallen. Elisha wrapped him in the blanket and hefted him over his shoulder. When he went outside with his burden, Madeline had already opened the rear doors of the hearse. Elisha lowered Roderick into the empty coffin and shut the lid then she closed the doors.

Tense moments passed as the rode to the cemetery, but they encountered nobody.

Hauling on the reins to stop the carriage a little way beyond the freshly dug grave, Elisha engaged the brake on the wheels and stood, surveying the immediate area. Still nobody in sight. He climbed down.

First, they slid Roderick's coffin out, since it was on top. Its foot hit the packed earth at the head of the grave. Exerting all his strength, Elisha pushed the head of the coffin and it slipped over the edge, falling into the six-foot deep hole reserved for Mrs. McGill. It made a dull thudding sound as it hit the bottom; luckily, the coffin landed on its base, fitting the grave perfectly, displacing only a little soil from the sides.

They eased the second coffin out; this slid quite easily on the floor's fitted rollers.

It perched slantwise, the head resting on the edge of the hearse floor, the foot on the packed earth. Madeline unlatched the upper section, lifted it. The marshal's eyes were shut, the blood on his head congealed. "I thought so. He's still breathing," she said.

"Not for long," Elisha said.

She shut the lid, latched it.

Elisha heaved this coffin onto the packed earth and shoved it hard.

For a second its bulk seemed to sail in mid-air, then it fell, thudding heavily on top of the first coffin.

Without speaking, Elisha tramped over to the spade sticking out of a pile of earth at the foot of the grave and began shoveling soil into the hole. It made a slightly hollow noise as it hit the top of the wood casket.

"I wouldn't like to be in his shoes if he regains consciousness," Madeline said.

"Sometimes, my dear, you have too much imagination." He panted heavily as he shoveled dirt.

Finally, satisfied with the heaped mound of soil, he left the spade sticking up. Wiping his hands, he helped her clamber onto the front bucket-seat of the hearse.

"We must collect all the money and valuables from our hiding places," he said, driving back to the hotel. His ill-gotten gains were sequestered throughout the funeral parlor; hers were in the cellar.

* * *

Berenice tried with difficulty to control her breathing. She knew that there was limited air-space in the cavity. Small irony, but the fact they'd gagged her meant she was taking in less air than normal. She was surprised how rational she felt. Particularly when she knew poor dead Horace was so near to her. Already she detected the distinctive odor of a dead body.

Tears trailed over her cheeks; she let them.

That scratching sound would haunt her to the end of her days.

She started. Well, that wasn't likely to be so long, was it?

Straining ankles and wrists at her bonds, she found there was no give in them. She wasn't even capable of scratching the prefabricated wooden section; she certainly couldn't kick it. She could move her torso from side to side, but not much, and the action didn't seem to make much noise. She could try shouting, though it would doubtless be a muffled mumble.

For now, though, she must conserve her strength and her air until she heard somebody nearby. Perhaps a cleaner would come into the room. Would they think to look behind the wall? Or would they too assume the sound was made by vermin?

She sobbed, swamped by guilt, thinking yet again how she and Cash had made love next door, while ignoring the intermittent scratching sound made by Horace.

Her head ached with recurrent "what-might-have-beens." And her bladder felt full. She sensed the warm blush on her cheeks. Perhaps eventually she would be reduced to that indignity of relieving herself where she stood, but she must contain the urge for now.

CHAPTER TWELVE

WITNESS

Outside the grand entrance to the Lenore Casino, Miles identified the footprint and horse-track. There were three horses at the hitching rail. A quick scrutiny of the dusty ground told him the paint was the animal he'd tracked. He bent down and checked the fore-hoof of the paint. Yes, without a doubt. He'd found the ambusher's mount.

He climbed the entrance steps and approached the Chinese sentry with a sword at his belt. "Do you speak English?" he asked.

"Yes, sir." A deadpan face. "Can I help you?"

He pointed to the paint. "Do you know who owns that horse?"

"Yes, sir. Mr. Usher Corman. It has a distinctive color."

"Thanks. Is he inside?"

"He should be, sir, but I have only recently come on duty here. The horse was there when I took my post."

"Thanks." He pushed on the door-handle.

"Sir, do you have business inside?" the sentry asked, his voice raised.

Half-turning, Miles folded back his lapel, showed the badge. "I'm a U.S. Marshal on official business. Is that good enough?"

"Yes, sir." The sentry bowed. "Excuse me for asking."

"No problem." He opened the door and entered the lavish atrium.

His appearance elicited the occasional stare from passing men and women, all of them smartly attired. He removed his hat, held it by his side, and then spotted another Chinese man who seemed to be supervising waiters and walked up to him.

"Sir, can I help you?" Another inscrutable face.

They sure sang from the same hymn sheet, he thought. "I'm Marshal Miles and I'm looking for a Mr. Usher Corman."

The immobile face transformed into a wide smile and the man's stiff posture relaxed. "Marshal Miles! It is an honor to meet you!" He grabbed Miles's hand and pumped it vigorously.

"But I don't know you," Miles said.

"No, sir, but I know you. My name is Wang Hulin." He gently touched Miles's elbow and led him to one side of the staircase. "You helped my cousin, Feng."

Miles smiled at the memory. "Feng could handle himself well enough, I noticed. It was an unfair fight, I reckoned, so I stepped in."

"You are most correct, sir. Our family is in your debt."

"Don't mention it, Hulin. Just tell me where I can find Mr. Corman."

Hulin's eyes lowered. "We try to remain discreet in our adopted country. But sometimes, we must speak."

"Go on. I'm listening."

"Mr. Corman was engaged in a secret affair with … the baron's wife …"

"That's not against the law, Hulin. I'm after Corman for something far more serious."

"Yes, but her death was not due to sleep-walking."

"Did Corman …?"

"No." Hulin glanced left and right, and then pointed up the staircase. "Go and see Lanying," he whispered archly. "She is in charge of the celestial women who work here. Her office is there."

Shaking Hulin's hand, Miles left and ascended the staircase.

Along the landing were several unmarked doors. Finally, he reached one that said *Chatelaine.* He knocked and a woman's voice responded with "Come in!"

A short stout Chinese woman stood in the middle of the office facing a slightly taller and thinner female waitress; she'd seen Miles out of the corner of her eye but didn't acknowledge him. Both women were dressed in unflattering long black robes with gold trim. The stout woman also wore a belt from which dangled a large key ring. She said, "You may go, Meifeng. And remember what I told you."

"Yes, mistress," the younger woman said and glided through a side door; it closed silently.

"Lanying?" Miles queried.

"Yes …?" Her ivory face was without emotion, not even a crease of enquiry, as if carved from ivory in fact; and there was coldness in her dark eyes.

"Hulin downstairs directed me to see you."

"And you are?"

"Marshal Miles."

Amazingly, her face altered, became soft, no longer stern, and her eyes lit up. "You are welcome, Marshal. Please sit. Do you want refreshment?" She sat on the edge of a nearby chair, knees together, poised, attentive.

"No thanks. I'm looking for Usher Corman, but that brought up a delicate subject... Hulin suggested there was something you could divulge about the death of the baron's wife."

Lanying lowered her eyes. "I do not know what happened, Marshal," she said in a soft whisper. "But I do know what did not happen." She raised her dark liquid eyes to his. "Lenore rode from here with her husband that night. I had been awake late into the night, nursing one of our female staff who was very ill. As I came from the sick room, I saw them both leave in the early morning. She was wearing her nightgown …"

"Did you see either return?"

"No, I went back to my charge and slept in a chair the rest of the night."

Miles leaned forward. "What time was her body found?"

"About five hours later, I think. It was early. Six o'clock."

"Who found her body?"

"A lawyer who was visiting the baron on business."

"Would that be Rufus Wilmot, by any chance?"

She gave a little start. "Yes, it was. Do you know him?"

"We've met. He has a habit of tripping over dead bodies, it now seems."

"I do not follow you, Marshal."

"Never mind, I was thinking aloud, Lanying." He stood abruptly. "I reckon I'll have a chat with the baron now."

She jerked out of her chair. "You will not say I told you this?"

"He doesn't need to know how I obtained the information, but I will use it." He took her tiny hand in his. "Thank you for your confidence."

* * *

Madeline warily descended the steps and entered the cellar. The lantern was still alight, casting long shadows. The salesman Willard Frey was where they'd left him, slumped in the chair.

She trod tentatively up to him. His wrists were rubbed raw in a vain attempt at escape. His chest rose and fell, breathing very shallow. She cast a glance at the bottom of the stairs. They wouldn't have time to move Frey now. That plan was stillborn. Steeling herself, she moved to the back of the chair and tipped it toward her, idly noticing that Frey was starting to go bald. She took the weight, suspended on the two rear legs of the chair.

Slowly, she dragged the chair backward toward the racks of wine.

Turning a corner, she pulled the chair a little further along an aisle of racks and then stopped, breathless with the exertion. Here would do, since this section of the cellar was rarely used; the most common wines were near the steps. Roderick had planned to sell the older vintages for a vast profit some years hence. Another plan stillborn.

She left Frey sitting unconscious and made her way to the tasting bench on the far wall. Here, she pulled out a couple of drawers. At the back, in a recess, they'd hidden stolen money and jewellery, all in leather pouches. Enough to finance another place and start again.

She licked her lips. Elisha had the taste for murder and robbery, after all.

She eyed the lantern and briefly wondered if she should set the place ablaze. Cover their tracks; the alcohol would feed the flames.

Yes, why not? She grabbed the lantern and flung it at the nearest rack.

The glass shattered, the flames poured out, igniting the spilt oil, and licked the wooden framework.

Carrying the pouches, she climbed the steps.

* * *

Cash remembered now, right up to that explosion. He reckoned it was Madeline Allan who fired a revolver, very close to his head. Had he been the target? Not likely. No, he recalled the argument. The revelation about the unsavory relationship the twins enjoyed. No, she'd been shooting at Roderick. Or had the second shot been intended to silence him, since he was the law and a witness? If so, then she was a lousy shot.

At risk of dislocating a shoulder, Cash had moved his hand down to his holster. It was empty. But they hadn't bothered to remove it and he located by touch a number of bullets.

For now, he gingerly removed two and raised them to his chest. Still by feel as he wanted to conserve his matches, he strained his fingertips to pry open the shell from the cartridge. He gently poured the gunpowder onto his chest, and repeated the process with the second bullet.

Licking his finger, he dipped the tip in the powder. By memory he found the join of the lid above his chest and traced it. He wondered if any of her funeral party had bothered to view him. Would they knowingly bury him alive? They wouldn't care; it would save a bullet.

Patiently, he packed gunpowder in the join to the right; he'd seen enough coffins in his time to recall the catch was situated there.

Satisfied with his efforts, even if he couldn't view the result, he lit a match and placed it where he'd packed the gunpowder.

The explosion was small, but the sound in this confined space was deafening. He'd be surprised if he hadn't got ruptured ear-drums.

Coughing on the smoke, he moved his right hand and pressed his palm against the ceiling where the powder had exploded. It lifted, just a fraction, but enough for him to be convinced that the latch was blown.

Gasping now, because he now had a lot less air than before the explosion, he braced his shoulders and pushed hard.

Yes! The lid raised a little more!

He stopped, eased it down again.

Traditional graves were six feet under. The depth of the coffin was about two feet. So that meant he had to push up through four feet of earth. Sure, it was loose, not compacted or hardened by drought yet. It wasn't wet, since there'd been no rain recently. Wet soil would be heavier than dry.

He almost baulked at the prospect.

The alternatives were bleak.

He had to try.

Or die trying.

CHAPTER THIRTEEN

THE BARON

Lanying had told Miles that the baron was presently in his private rooms. Miles found the door further along the landing, almost directly opposite the swinging pendulum. A Chinese short thick-set sentry stood to one side of the door, a sword sheathed at his belt. The sentry bowed. "You have an appointment, sir?"

"No. I'm a U.S. Marshal and I want to speak to the baron."

The sentry moved a step sideways to block the door. "Baron von Kempelen only sees people with an appointment, sir." Obstructive yet polite.

"The law doesn't need an appointment. Go in and tell him I want to see him. Pronto!"

Perhaps it was his tone, or the glare he gave, but the sentry bowed slightly, turned and knocked on the door then opened it.

"What is it, Teng?" A faint foreign inflection, laced with irritation.

"A U.S. Marshal to see you, Baron. He does not have an appointment."

"Then tell him to make one with my secretary."

Miles elbow-barged the sentry to one side, slickly sliding the sword from its scabbard as he slipped through. "I've got an appointment now, Baron!" He leveled the point of the blade on Teng's throat.

The baron was alone. He adjusted his monocle and stood up from a sofa, calmly lowering a newspaper to the seat. A curtain-edged wide window behind him overlooked a great expanse of land beyond. "What is the meaning of this intrusion, sir?"

"I'm a U.S. Marshal on official business. I don't need an appointment. I need answers to my questions."

"I do not like your manners, Marshal." The baron shrugged. "Since you're here, I suppose I can spare you a little time." He gestured at an armchair near the sofa.

"I'll stand, thanks."

"You may go, Teng," the baron said.

"My sword …?"

Miles glared. "I'll return it when I've finished our little chat. Now beat it, Teng, like your boss says!"

He'd estimated that the girth and weight of Teng suggested the man wasn't adept at that slick unarmed combat employed by the miner Wang Feng in town. Teng probably relied on his bulk, or the sword, to bully his way through life. Teng bowed and left, closing the door behind him.

Moving round the sofa, the baron sauntered nonchalantly to the drinks cabinet on the right. Three swords of different types hung on the wall above the cabinet; Miles recognized the rapier, but not the others.

The baron poured a finger of brandy into a goblet. "Do you require a drink, Marshal? Breaking into people's private rooms can be thirsty work, I imagine."

"No, I need a clear head to get round the problem I have."

Facing him now, the baron sipped his drink and leaned against the cabinet. "What is your problem?"

"You employ two people I'm interested in."

"Oh, who might they be?"

"Usher Corman and Rufus Wilmot."

* * *

Elisha hauled on the reins of the buckboard and halted at the entrance steps to *The Bells*. Madeline rushed onto the veranda carrying several leather pouches and a suitcase. Then she halted, mouth open in surprise. "You've got the buckboard!"

"The hearse was a mite conspicuous," he said. "Have you got all you want? Enough!"

He peered through the open doorway. Smoke issued under the cellar door. "What have you done?"

"I thought it best to burn the place down." She stopped, cocked her head. "That is the thing to do, isn't it?"

Most sensible of her, he thought. He smiled thinly. "Yes, that's for the best." He climbed down. "I'll help with the case. Then we should get some provisions from the kitchen—just in case."

"All right." She hurried inside, glancing furtively at the gushing smoke. The kitchen was to the left of the lounge. Elisha was by her side and they stacked tins of food into a small crate and he carried it to the buckboard.

She pointed at two big crates on the flatbed. "You've brought a couple of slot-machines, I see."

"Yes, we can sell them on later."

"What did Jerry say about that?"

"Poor Jerry won't be saying anything to anybody," Elisha said somberly.

"Oh, a pity. He was a nice boy." She wrapped her arm around his. "We're burning our bridges, aren't we?"

"Indeed, Maddy. Literally." He helped her up to the front seat and sat beside her. "We will have a new start."

"But where?"

"To begin with, I believe we should hide at Bryan."

"Why the ghost town?"

"Nobody will think to look for us there."

"Who will be looking for us?" She reached into the well under the seat, brought out a rifle. "We're simply eloping ..."

He jerked the reins and the horse walked on. "There are too many missing persons now, my dear. The marshal's absence will draw attention. And of course when Mrs. McGill's body isn't collected, further questions will be asked."

"Not to mention young Jerry's body ..."

"Quite. Sadly, one unfortunate thing has led to another." He tut-tutted. "All unintended consequences."

She half-turned in the seat, watched the hotel. The flames hadn't taken hold yet, though she could detect a small cloud of smoke issuing at the base of the western wall. "Yes, you're right, of course."

He patted her hand. "When the hue-and-cry dies down, we will go north."

* * *

Berenice's legs felt numb and weak, pins and needles jangled up her thighs, while her wrists were sore, taking some of her body weight. Her stomach was queasy; fear playing havoc with her nerves, no doubt. Considering her predicament, she marveled that she was still lucid.

She blinked at darkness, shocked at detecting slight movement.

And then she gasped, sucking against the gag, starting a brief paroxysm of coughing.

She couldn't see it in the dark, but she could feel its body brushing over her feet; she was thankful she wore boots.

Sweat soaked her clothing now, and her face felt flushed, but she couldn't do anything to wipe away the irritating wetness.

Rats. Her brother's dead body. Slowly suffocating. In complete darkness. In almost absolute silence. She was in a living nightmare. But the living aspect of it would not last much longer, she feared.

She wondered how Horace met his end. Did he simply lose consciousness through lack of air? Or did he go insane first, screaming against his gag? She shuddered and a cold horripilation traced her flesh.

* * *

Baron von Kempelen made a dismissive gesture. "Corman is useful from time to time, but of no great importance."

"And the lawyer?" Miles prompted.

"Mr. Wilmot has been most helpful dealing with the legal matters pertaining to this complex. He is important to me, I must admit."

Raising the sword to rest on his shoulder, Miles took a couple of paces closer to the baron. "I'm curious. Why haven't you asked me for the reason I'm interested in those two men."

Von Kempelen shrugged. "I thought you would get around to it eventually. I must admit I cannot comprehend what interest they have for you."

"You 'admit' a lot, without admitting anything, Baron. Let me explain. Corman bushwhacked me on the road to Rock Springs. I was escorting a prisoner."

The baron gulped his brandy. "Are you sure?"

"I tracked his horse here."

"Inconclusive, I suspect. Perhaps his horse was borrowed. I cannot comprehend why he would attack you, Marshal."

"On the face of it the idea seems incomprehensible, doesn't it?"

"What of Mr. Wilmot? Surely he hasn't attacked you as well?"

"No, but I need to question him further about his witness statement over the death of the postmaster at Rock Springs."

"Ah, yes." The baron pursed his lips, and then added, "I had heard of that sad event. Mr. Wilmot told me during his last visit."

"So he comes out here regularly, does he?"

"Yes. As I told you, he deals with the legal paperwork." He gestured at the window. "You may have noticed on your way in, I have great plans for this place."

"I'm wondering if there's a connection ..."

"What connection, Marshal? I do not understand."

"Wilmot happened on the warm corpse of the postmaster and some time before he happened on the body of your wife Lenore ..."

At mention of his wife's name, the baron's face briefly twisted in an ugly rictus and the monocle popped out. He gulped the rest of the brandy. "I do not think she has any bearing on your investigations, Marshal."

"Is that so? Actually, I'm *very* interested in the facts surrounding the death of your wife."

Two bright red spots appeared on the baron's cheeks. "The affair was investigated at the time. The sheriff was most understanding. It was an unfortunate *accident*."

"In her nightdress." Miles pointed the sword at the window. "Out there. In the dark hours of the morning …"

"Will you stop pointing that weapon? You clearly don't know the first thing about handling a sword!"

"Whereas you do, is that it?" Miles taunted, jabbing the sword point toward the wall display over the drinks cabinet.

Von Kempelen curled his upper lip. "I wear my dueling scar with pride, Marshal."

"I trust the other guy got worse?"

"Do not be flippant, Marshal. Dueling is a serious business."

"Sure, Baron." Miles lowered the sword, tapped its point on the carpet. "Back to my business. Tell me about your wife Lenore."

The scar tissue on the baron's face seemed to darken and his free eye narrowed. "There is nothing to tell. I have asked you politely not to talk about her!"

"Why? Don't you want to remember her?"

"Of course I do!" the baron spluttered. Hand shaking, he gestured vaguely, "I—I built a mausoleum for her! I named this place after her!"

"And every time you ride through the entrance arch you see her name."

"Precisely!"

"So why won't you talk about her death?"

"It—it is too awful, too tragic. For her to die at—at a young age, and so beautiful a creature …" The baron let out a sob and returned to the drinks cabinet.

"Where did you go with her the night of her death?"

The baron slopped brandy, some of it missing his glass. "What—what do you mean?"

"You were seen riding with Lenore in the early hours. She was in her nightdress. What was so urgent that she didn't have time to change?"

Shaking his head, the baron said, "You—you are mistaken. I don't know where these scurrilous lies have originated, but they are not worthy of an answer!"

"I believe you lured her—probably with a tall tale about her lover being hurt on the trail …"

"How could you …? How dare you!" He glared, and then flung the half-full glass at Miles. Swiftly, he swiveled round, reached up and snatched the rapier from the wall. "I have heard enough! You besmirch her name!"

"Lenore?"

"Stop saying that!" His complexion reddened.

Miles persisted in goading. "Lenore had a lover, but you never found out who it was, did you? She didn't tell you before she died, did she?"

Without warning, without replying, the baron lunged with the rapier.

Miles barely managed to side-step, the thin blade piercing the hem of his jacket.

He tossed the sword to his left hand and reached for his revolver, but the baron's rapier point jabbed his hand as the gun came free of its holster and he dropped it. Hissing with the sudden pain, he swore. Damn, the baron was good!

Hefting Teng's sword in his left hand, Miles parried with the big blade though he found it difficult; he couldn't use his right, since it was covered in blood and painful. Keeping that nasty point at bay was like trying to swat a gnat with a cleaver.

Backing toward the door, he slapped the deadly rapier away repeatedly.

"You Americans are all the same!" the baron snarled. "Rush in and bluster, relying on force rather than finesse! I will show you German finesse as I cut you to ribbons!"

The rapier point slashed at Miles's jacket, cutting away a lapel and part of the breast section, baring the badge pinned to his shirt.

He's toying with me, Miles realized.

At that moment, the door which was now to his right opened and Teng stood there, a concerned look on his face. "Baron, I heard—"

The baron lunged and in the same instant Miles grabbed Teng and hauled the man in front of him as a shield. The rapier sank deep into Teng's back. Life deserted the impassive face at once. Miles dropped him.

Screaming unintelligibly, the baron pulled his blade free while Miles ducked out the doorway onto the landing.

A few people on either side backed off, some of them exclaiming in shock as the baron jumped over Teng's corpse and time after time thrust his bloody blade at Miles.

His sword deflecting the rapier, Miles backed into the bannister with nowhere else to retreat.

CHAPTER FOURTEEN

MAUSOLEUM

Cash ripped silk from the lining of the coffin, a big enough piece for his purpose. He had no elbow room to fasten a mere strip over his mouth and nose and tie it at the back of his head, so he settled for a sort of hood.

Breathing in deeply, trying to suck in as much air as his lungs could stand, he manoeuvred the hood over his head and, bracing his shoulders, heaved with all his might against the upper portion of the coffin lid.

Slowly, very slowly it moved up, displacing soil that trickled into the gap.

He kept breathing while there was air, the silk filtering it, topping up his lungs, at each breath pushing harder.

He heard and felt clumps of soil falling into the gap he made. Fear gave him added strength. His forearm muscles strained. He was still breathing air, but now soil was brushing against the silk hood, trickling down his neck, blocking his ears.

As he shoved upward, he sidled along the length of the coffin, so that his torso began to emerge from the opening.

Pressure of soil weighed on his chest, the silk over his face was now completely covered with earth, and his nostrils were clogged with the musty rank smell. He mustn't cough!

He held his breath and continued to push, constantly, using the lid portion of the coffin like a door, persistently pressing against an unforgiving weight.

Blind though he was, bright lights flashed before his eyes. He kept pushing and moving his body along the confines of the coffin, like a contortionist from a traveling circus. He'd heard that escapologists dislocated their shoulders to get out of tight holes. Right now, all he wanted was more air.

He used both hands now, scooping earth from above, directing it down both sides of him, as if swimming in treacle; it was probably not as tacky; still, the soil clung.

He sensed his legs emerge from the coffin, his right knee banging on the lip of the opening, and still he strained to swim upward.

Seconds that spanned into a lifetime. His lifetime soon to be cut short.

Yet when his air was virtually gone, his up-thrusting hands met no resistance.

Frantically, as his air was giving out, he burst up from the earth and gasped. And breathed. Coughing, choking on the filthy silk, feeling the grittiness of small particles of soil in his mouth, he pulled it away and gulped in fresh air. He seemed frozen there, only his head, shoulders and arms above the grave's soil, but he didn't care. Because he could breathe.

Craning his neck round, soil fell away from him. It was early evening, he reckoned. He was on the edge of the cemetery; he'd ridden past this very grave earlier today.

He knew he was in a sort of sitting position, his feet at the lip of the coffin opening. For some reason, the grave wasn't six feet deep; he knew that if it had been, he wouldn't have managed to get out. His breath would have expired long before.

After that somber realization, his first thought was for Berenice.

If these people were capable of burying him alive, then what had they done to her?

And why? Over a lover's triangle?

Right now, it didn't matter.

When he'd caught his breath, he wriggled and fought his way out of the clinging soil.

* * *

Brushing the earth from his clothing, Cash stood next to his grave and sensed a chill shiver crawl over his flesh. What a terrible fate, almost buried alive. Abruptly, he bent over and vomited, disgorging his food and bile and soil.

When his stomach stopped heaving and he no longer retched, he straightened and set off for the hotel. But his legs were a little shaky. He'd probably strained a muscle or two while contorting his body and constantly pushing against the earth. Although he wanted to run, he only managed a fast unsteady walk.

Finally, he climbed the entrance steps, trailing small clods of soil.

Entering the foyer, he froze. Smoke seeped from under the cellar door. Great gouts of smoke. He rushed in an ungainly gait to the door and leaned against it to listen. He jerked away, the wood was so hot. He heard the crackling of flames.

What if Berenice was down there?

The handle was too hot, so he kicked in the door and was immediately pummeled by a massive draught of hot air. Tongues of flame flicked at him, singeing his eyebrows. He stumbled backward and experienced an oppressive sense of loss pressing on his chest. If anybody was in that cellar, they were dead.

Though he feared he was grasping at straws, he decided he must try her room again. If she wasn't there, perhaps there was a clue leading to her whereabouts.

His mouth was dry, gritty. He crossed to the lounge, grabbed a carafe of water and drank some, washed his mouth out and spat on the floor. He noticed the blood-stained carpet near the counter. Madeline and Elisha hadn't bothered to conceal it. This suggested they were not planning on staying, and had set the place alight.

Lying under a chair was his Colt. He must have drawn it instinctively when Madeline fired the first shot, but the second shot had been too fast. He picked it up, glad of its weighty reassuring feel, and slipped it into its holster.

He found a bottle of brandy and took a good swig. The liquor burned his mouth and throat and he felt better almost immediately as it warmed his gut.

He swiveled round and headed for the stairs.

Ignoring the aches in his legs, he raced along the corridor.

Berenice's door was still locked.

Bracing himself, he kicked it in.

No hotel guests emerged from other rooms. He hesitated, thinking he should warn them the hotel was on fire. No, first, he needed to find Berenice!

He entered her room but didn't bother to shut the door after him.

His heart sank. Nausea hit him again, but his stomach had nothing to throw up. The bed clothes were disordered, but the bed was empty. Her two carpetbags were on the small table at the foot of the bed, and her blue satin dress hung from a wardrobe door. He walked over to it, caught the scent she'd worn; was that only last night?

He opened the tallboy's drawers and found a few undergarments. He checked the contents of her bags. "I travel light," she'd said. He'd joked that his idea of traveling light and hers differed considerably.

Her riding-skirt and blouse were missing. He should have gone to see if the chestnut was still in the stables. Maybe young Jerry would know where she'd gone. If he hurried there now, he might still be in time.

Turning toward the door, he was surprised to see the black cat, Pluto. It wasn't purring but making a strange almost plaintive sound as it brushed its side against the far wall of the room. Then it lifted its head, stared at him; those bright green eyes seemed imbued with intelligence.

"You miss her too, eh, Pluto?"

He leant down to pick him up.

The cat snarled, baring its teeth, squirmed and jumped out of his hands.

Then it scratched at the wall, meowing.

A muted mumbling sounded as if it came from behind the wall.

What the hell?

"Who's there?" he asked and then swore. *Who else could it be, idiot!* "Berenice!"

The mumbling was louder now, and a scraping rubbing noise accompanied it.

Hurrying out of the room, he ran to the head of the stairs and grabbed the fire axe off the wall. Running along the corridor now, he banged the axe head on the doors as he passed, shouting, "Fire! Fire!"

Two doors opened and men looked out. "What's the ruckus?"

Heading for Berenice's door, Cash said, "Get everyone out! There's a fire in the cellar!" And then he was inside her room again.

Despite the new commotion of hotel guests banging doors and rushing about, Cash could hear the rubbing and mumbling sounds. Judging where they came from, he measured a pace or so to the right and wielded the axe, cutting into the wall.

Wood splintered.

He chopped at the wall until he could see there was a cavity before the wall beyond.

Though his limbs ached, he chopped, discarding lengths of wood to the floor.

And then he saw her, to his left, her arm upraised, wrist tied to a batten. Her fingers moved. She was alive!

Now he chopped with purpose.

Before long, he had removed the section of wall partition to reveal Berenice entirely.

He unfastened her gag and she sobbed, tears trailing over grime-covered cheeks. Her eyes showed shock at his appearance. He supposed he was covered in dirt.

He withdrew the knife from his boot and cut her bonds and she fell into his arms.

* * *

Usher Corman clutched his hat to his aching chest and let tears run down his unshaven face as he stood in front of the mausoleum. Even after all this time, he couldn't understand why she was there in her nightdress, all alone. Sleep-walking? She'd never mentioned she did that. But if she'd been asleep, she wouldn't know, would she? It was bad enough that she was dead. It was much worse to think that she'd been torn apart by a pack of wolves. He'd dearly wanted to join the baron to hunt wolves when he learned of her death, but the boss wanted to do it alone and he couldn't muster a valid argument to join him. Now, for the hundredth time he vowed that as long as he lived he would never forget Lenore.

"Mr. Corman, sir!" one of the Chinamen called, running toward him.

Hurriedly wiping his face, Corman swung round and put his hat on. "What is it, Wang?"

"It's the boss, sir, he's fighting the marshal with swords!"

"What? Marshal?" His blood ran cold. Somehow, Miles must have tracked me here, he thought. Damn Wilmot, I shouldn't have listened to him!

If the marshal killed the baron, I'm out of a job. He smiled briefly. Not that the baron was likely to lose, if they really were using swords. Still, I'd better go and make sure the marshal *does* lose. Because if the marshal won, he'd come looking for me!

"All right, Weng, I'll come with you."

Without casting a last look at the mausoleum to his lost love, he jogged after Weng Hulin.

They arrived in the atrium as the fight was reaching its climax.

Corman stopped and gazed upward at the landing, drawn by the clash of steel.

Swords it was, then; so the baron was going to win.

CHAPTER FIFTEEN

PENDULUM AND PIT

A look of triumph washed over the baron's features. He laughed, his mouth wide.

And Miles flung his badge directly into the baron's gaping maw.

Von Kempelen's eyes started, the monocle dropping on its gold chain, dangling at his chest, as he choked on the metal. With his free hand the baron tried removing the badge, gagging all the while.

Miles followed with a slicing action that severed the baron's sword hand completely from its wrist. Blood spurted everywhere and people screamed. Out of the corner of his eye he saw a woman faint.

Pushing forward, ignoring the baron's cries of pain and the screams of the onlookers, Miles dropped his sword and grabbed the baron's shirt. Heaving him off the landing floor, he flung von Kempelen over the bannister rail.

Arms and legs gyrating, the baron seemed to fly across the intervening space and, by chance, he landed on the massive bob or weight at the end of the pendulum's rod. Frantically, he held on with one hand and wrapping his legs round the thick metal.

The pendulum swing was immediately slowed by the additional weight.

Above, the mechanism groaned and the clock emitted strange unfamiliar sounds, pinging, screeching.

Without warning, the rod separated from the clock and the pendulum and the baron plummeted.

* * *

It happened too fast. Corman instinctively dived out of the way, but he was too slow, too late. The bob crushed Corman's skull but its fall was not arrested by mere flesh and bone.

The weight of the pendulum's rod and bob combined with that of the baron and Corman created a small pit in the atrium's expensive marble tile.

* * *

Cash stood with an arm round Berenice's shoulders, watching the flames licking the woodwork of the window of her room. Her tears washed away some of the grime and smoke on her cheeks. With an automatic motion, she stroked the black cat in her arms, her frame racked by sobbing.

There'd been no time to free her brother's body. Cash had managed to grab one carpetbag, flung some of her clothes in, and then took her to his room and retrieved his rifle and saddle-bags. They'd staggered down the stairs only minutes before the staircase was engulfed by the encroaching fire.

Beside them gathered other hotel guests, many of them distressed, for most of their belongings were presently being incinerated.

"Madeline and Elisha aren't here," Cash said, observing the crowd.

He'd already told her about the death of Roderick and his own premature burial. But the demise of one of her tormentors had little effect. She was in a daze, clutching onto the black cat.

Earlier, he'd spotted the tracks of a wagon beyond the hotel, leading roughly north-west.

Gently, he led Berenice away toward the stables, her steps unsteady.

Fortunately, the burning hotel hadn't spread to the adjacent buildings.

"Wait here," he whispered as they reached the stable door.

Inside, he noticed one of Frey's crates, upended and broken, the gleaming slot-machine poking through the split wood. The buckboard had gone, so now he knew which vehicle had created those tracks.

As he feared, he found young Jerry lying dead in an empty stall. He covered the lad with a horse-blanket. He gritted his teeth; there was no call to kill the poor boy. He hadn't realized until now, but the boy reminded him of his days in Bowler Gillicuddy's livery. Heavy of heart, he walked over to his horse and spotted Berenice's chestnut. It didn't take him long to saddle both.

The black cat persisted in staying with her, sometimes riding on the rump of the chestnut, sometimes running alongside. Berenice seemed to gain a little comfort in its presence, even if the animal had belonged to the Allans.

For a good distance, they rode in silence, death an unwelcome companion.

* * *

Miles strolled onto the station platform. He'd changed his shirt and retrieved his badge from the baron's mouth. He hadn't found time to replace the torn jacket, though. It could wait.

He quickly identified Rufus Wilmot waiting with a suitcase and a small satchel.

"Fancy meeting you here, Mr. Wilmot," he said, stepping in front of the lawyer.

Wilmot's eyes widened. "Marshal Miles, this is a surprise. Are you returning to Cheyenne?" He glanced about. "Not escorting your prisoner?"

"Mr. Raven has been released without charge, sir."

"Really?" He chuckled. "Well, that's good for him, I suppose ..."

"I've just come from Casino Lenore."

"Oh? And how is the baron?"

"Deceased."

"Pardon? Did you say he's dead?"

"I did. I killed him."

Color drained from the lawyer's face. "In self-defense, I suppose?"

"Yes. He broke under questioning and went berserk—but before he died he told me a few things …"

"Sort of death-bed confession, is that it."

"You tend to stumble onto death, don't you, Mr. Wilmot?"

"How do you mean?"

"First there was Clemm, the postmaster. And then the baron's wife, Lenore."

Wilmot bit his lip, his eyes evading Miles's direct stare. "He told you, did he?"

"Yes. Care to fill in the blanks?"

"How much do you know?"

"Enough, Mr. Wilmot. Enough to prevent you from catching the train."

The transition from supreme confidence to abject defeat was sudden. Wilmot seemed to deflate in front of him.

"It's as the baron said. I found the body of Lenore, but the baron had been careless and left evidence that he'd been there. I concealed the evidence and suggested he might want to repay me for my efforts. Is that what he told you?"

"It is," Miles lied.

"I don't blame him, I suppose … Yes, the baron knew his wife was having an affair but he didn't know the man's identity... That night, he concocted a story about him having a fight with her lover, taking care not to name him. He told her he'd left her lover badly wounded on the trail, but now he felt remorse and wanted to redeem himself."

131

"Crafty fellow, wasn't he? He wanted her to let slip her lover's name?"

"Yes. But she never said his name though! She believed him and they rode out at once. I don't think he intended to kill her, but when they were so far along the trail, he knocked her off her horse." Wilmot closed his eyes briefly, and shook his head at what must have been an unpleasant memory. "At that moment I'm sure the baron was insane with jealousy." He opened his eyes, pain in them. "It was terrible. He used a knife to cut out her cheating heart ..."

"And," Miles added, "left her for the wolves."

"Yes."

"But you couldn't bring yourself to tell the sheriff."

"I deal in the law, Marshal. There was no proof." He shuddered. "The wolves had chewed her so much there wasn't any evidence of a knife cut." Wilmot's lips curled. "You can't arrest me for this. There were no witnesses. It's your word against mine. I hear the train coming."

"You won't be getting on it, as I said before."

"I told you, you have no proof I blackmailed the baron."

Miles half-turned and signaled to the stationmaster standing outside the waiting room. Three Chinese men walked onto the platform and bowed briefly, then stood watching.

"Those three witnesses have come forward and identified you as the supplier of opium to the celestials."

"This is preposterous!" He spat on the platform. "They're Chinese!"

"You were in the post office collecting your latest consignment but it had broken open and Mr. Clemm noticed and accused you. So you had no choice but to kill him and then ran out the back. Lucky for you, or so you thought, you spotted Vincent Raven going inside. Before Raven could raise the alarm, you jumped at the opportunity to frame him."

"It's conjecture."

"Not with three witnesses. And a bullet."

"Bullet?"

"You got Usher Corman to ambush me and Raven. You knew I was digging around and might find an incriminating connection."

"More dubious facts?" His laugh sounded hollow. "What about the bullet?"

"I'm pretty sure the bullet dug from Raven's shoulder will match the rifling of Corman's weapon, which was retrieved from his horse outside the Lenore casino."

"But that incriminates Corman, not me! He's lying if he implicates me. I warned him ..." Wilmot stopped, bit his lip. "I've got nothing more to say."

* * *

While washing the dishes, Gwendolyn peered out the kitchen window. "Vincent, somebody's coming!"

He rose from the table, puffing on his pipe, walked up to her and looked over her shoulder. "A buckboard? Who'd want to come here?"

"They might want to buy a horse or two?"

Teeth clenching on the pipe stem, he grinned. "It's about time our luck changed, Gwen!"

She wiped her hands on a towel and fussed with her hair. "I'll put fresh java on the stove."

"Yeah, you do that. I'll go welcome them."

He went to the door, opened it and stopped, staring.

The buckboard wasn't slowing down. It trundled past their ramshackle building and headed into the middle of the ghost town's main street. There was a man and a woman on the seat, a small amount of luggage and two very large wooden crates on the flatbed.

He scratched his head. *What were they doing here?*

"Coffee's on!" Gwen called.

Instinct impelled him to silently shut the door. "Quiet, Gwen!"

"Landsakes, what's gotten into you?"

"I don't like it."

"What?"

"They didn't notice our corral; they rode straight on by, heading for the center of town."

"But there's nothing there. Nobody. We're the town, we're all there is."

He puffed on his pipe. "I don't think they're the sociable type. I reckon they've chosen to come here to *hide*."

* * *

Elisha steered the buckboard round the rear of the dilapidated Annabel Lee Saloon and halted by the rear entrance. Several paces from the door stood a well, its bucket tipped on its side. The glass in the windows on the second storey was unbroken, which boded well.

"Let's hope they've got a spare bed, eh?" He winked.

She shuddered. "I don't fancy sleeping here."

"Well, we have no choice at present." He thumbed over his shoulder. "Unless you want to sleep in that ramshackle shack we passed on the way in."

"What's the difference? All these places are old and falling apart!"

"That shack is occupied by a Negro. I saw him on the stoop as we drove by."

She gasped. "But he'll be a witness. He could tell people we're here!"

"That thought crossed my mind as well." Elisha shook his head. "I'd hoped the town would be deserted. Lord's sake, it is a ghost town!"

"What're you going to do?"

"Let's check inside the saloon first." He jumped down and offered her a hand. "Coming?"

"Oh, all right."

As they skirted the well, he peered down. "There's water." He dropped the bucket, heard it splash, and hauled it up. He cupped a hand and sipped the water. "It's all right, not stagnant at any rate." He spat on the ground.

The rear door was shut but not locked. It groaned on rusting hinges as he pushed it open. Brushing aside cobwebs with his hand, he walked inside. Madeline followed, a hand on his arm.

135

The sun's rays slanted through gaps in the walls and provided enough light to reveal the back room, overturned tables and chairs, and a couple of crates of dust-covered empty bottles.

He shoved open the door into the saloon area, a kind of atrium where the ceiling was badly damaged, sunlight percolating through. It was a large space that boasted a long bar on the left, tables and clusters of chairs, a card-table and a staircase leading to a landing. He crossed the floor with Madeline behind him, the floorboards creaking under their weight.

Treading over to the bar counter, Elisha went round and fumbled in several crates. He found a half-full bottle of brandy, uncorked it and smelled it. "Seems all right." Wiping the lip with a sleeve, he took a swig, and gasped. "Jesus, that's strong!" He offered her the bottle but she shook her head.

"To think I burned all that liquor!"

"It was unavoidable, my dear. We had to move fast, once you shot your dear brother."

"You don't blame me, do you?"

"No, of course not. He was throttling me, remember?"

Placing the brandy bottle on the counter, he said, "Let's inspect the accommodation, shall we?"

"If we must."

They climbed the staircase, the treads seeming to object at each step.

Finally, they reached the landing and went from bedroom to bedroom, and surprisingly at the farthest room along they found a bed that offered a clean though dusty mattress and a pile of sheets in a wardrobe. The ceiling seemed intact, with no stains from rain.

"Home, sweet home!" he said. "We've got water, provisions and a bed."

She turned up her lip. "It's a long time since I was reduced to this kind of life, Elisha. I don't know if I can handle it now."

He embraced her and pressed his lips on hers. Between kisses, he murmured, "Remember, we've got thousands of dollars to spend, once we get away." Her tongue probed his and he gasped for air, pulled away slightly, hands caressing her curves. "I promise you, when we move north, we'll live exceedingly well."

"I like the taste of that—and you," she purred and tugged at him and they both fell onto the mattress.

They were immediately engulfed in a cloud of dust and started coughing and laughing.

CHAPTER SIXTEEN

CEMETERY DANCE

Cash reined in on a crest of scrub land that overlooked the abandoned town of Bryan. Berenice eased her horse alongside him. Perched on her cantle, the black cat meowed.

To the left of the main street he saw a length of railroad track, most of it overgrown, and a lopsided water tank on its tall trestle, the hose dangling loose. On the right at the beginning of the main street stood a shack and a corral. Further to the right was the cemetery populated with an assortment of marble, granite and wood grave-markers.

"The buckboard tracks definitely lead there." He pointed "Past that shack. There are horses in the corral. I thought you said the place was abandoned."

"It is. I'll investigate."

"We'll both go," she said, withdrawing her Winchester.

"Wouldn't you like to think so?"

"I'm not in an arguing mood," she said. "I owe Mrs. Allan." She ratcheted a bullet into the barrel.

"All right. But we don't go charging in. We'll do this my way."

"Your way is fine by me. I reckon you owe Elisha Price."

"You'd be right there." He twisted in his saddle, observing the horizon. "It'll soon be dark. Let's get down to that shack."

Cash led them round to approach from the east, out of view from any of the buildings in the town's main street. Dusk was feathering the western sky as they drew up at the corner of the corral.

A Negro stepped away from the shack, a Greener shotgun cocked and ready. "State your business." Then he immediately lowered the weapon. "Sorry, Miss, I didn't recognize you!"

Berenice swung her leg over the saddle and slid off the chestnut. The black cat jumped to the ground and ran toward the shack. "Mr. Raven?" she exclaimed.

"That's me." He gave her a wide grin. "Marshal Miles released me without charge."

"Marshal Gideon Miles?" Cash queried.

"Yes, sir." Raven squinted at Cash. "Do you know him?"

Peeling back his jacket, Cash showed his badge. "I'm U.S. Marshal Cash Laramie. We're both from Cheyenne." He turned to Berenice. "You know each other?"

She smiled and explained briefly. "Sorry, I should have mentioned it, but since seeing your friend I've been somewhat distracted."

"And that's an understatement," Cash said. He dismounted and studied the horses in the corral. "Fine stock you have here, Mr. Raven."

"They're all legal. I've got bills of sale."

Cash held up a hand. "I don't doubt it. Can we go inside?"

"Yeah, sure, Marshal. My wife always has coffee brewing."

"Much obliged."

* * *

Cash was surprised how hungry he'd become. He cleared the plate of beans and hash, scooping the remains with bread, and washed it all down with two cups of java. He was amused to note that Berenice seemed as ravenous. At least the trauma of being tied behind a wall next to her murdered brother hadn't affected her will to live. He supposed her desire for revenge goaded her on. Maybe later, when it was all over—if they survived, he allowed—the shock would really hit her. He hoped he could be there for her if that happened.

It was dark by the time they'd eaten. He went out to the horses and rummaged in his saddle-bags for his moccasins and binoculars.

The full moon lent a ghostly aspect to the abandoned town as he peered along the main street. He returned, slid inside and sat down.

"It's all agreed, then?" He began replacing his boots with a pair of moccasins.

"Yes," Berenice said, disappointment in her tone. "But you only nose around … and then you'll come back for me." Meaningfully, she eyed her Winchester resting against the wall.

"That's it, a scouting trip." Grabbing his Yellow Boy, he offered her a grin and made for the door.

"Be careful," she called softly.

Closing the door quietly, he made his way across the street in a crouching run, his binoculars thudding against his chest. The night chorus of crickets filled the air.

He reached the remnants of the U.P. rail sidings and gingerly clambered up the water tower's ladder. At the top platform, he commanded a view of the entire town and surrounding area.

From this angle he could just distinguish a buckboard standing at the rear of the Annabel Lee Saloon. He raised the binoculars and scanned the upper storey of the saloon.

A light flickered in the farthest window.

* * *

Hastily dressing, Elisha sneezed. "I've been thinking. It's not a good idea to leave the man at that shack alive."

As she pulled the dress over her head, she said, "You were thinking about that while we—?"

"No, no, my dear. I was in paradise *then* …"

"When, then?"

"Before. As soon as I saw him, I guess."

She exhaled. "You're right, of course."

"He won't be expecting any trouble, I'm sure. It will be easy, over before he knows what happened." He fished in his suitcase and pulled out a gun-belt and holstered Smith & Wesson .45.

"When was the last time you used that?" she asked.

"A couple of months ago. One of Roddy's targets wouldn't stay dead, so I finished him off," he said coldly.

"I'll come with you." She grabbed the buckboard rifle.

"You don't need to."

She let out a short laugh. "I'm not staying here all alone."

"Yes, right."

Slowly, they descended the stairs into the deserted dilapidated saloon. "We'll go round the back way," he said. "The boardwalk probably squeaks too much and the street's too wide, we might be seen."

"Lead on," she whispered, expertly loading the rifle.

* * *

Cash decided he couldn't endanger Berenice. She'd been through enough. If he could, he'd take them alive. She'd get her revenge watching Madeline hang for her crimes.

Soundlessly, he clambered down the ladder.

His moccasins barely making any noise, he moved up the street, clinging to shadows, avoiding loose boards with instinct gleaned from his Arapaho upbringing.

He moved on the opposite side of the street past the saloon and then crossed the road, dashing to the concealment of a deserted haberdashery.

Treading with care, his back to the wood walls, he sidled toward the saloon's batwing doors.

Then he stopped and briefly stepped out onto the road. He glanced up.

The room light was still on. *Good.*

Swiftly, he ducked under the batwings, and slid over the floor. His left pant leg snagged a loose nail and tore, otherwise he was inside without mishap.

Regaining his feet, the rifle ready, he approached the foot of the staircase. It was the only way up. He'd be vulnerable here if either of them should come onto the landing with a weapon.

Silently, he climbed the stairs, keeping his feet to the left-hand side of the treads.

He reached the landing and released his pent-up breath.

The room with the lighted window was at the far end, to the right.

His mouth was dry as he walked along the landing on threadbare carpet.

He came to the door. Right now, he'd welcome Miles by his side. Over the years, they'd burst into more than enough rooms, coordinating their moves, covering each other.

Steady now, hold your breath, don't bother with the handle.

Bracing himself, he kicked in the door, and barked, "Don't move! U.S. Marshal!"

He was speaking to an empty room.

But this was definitely their hiding place. Cash recognized one of Madeline's dresses flung over a chair back. And to pile on Elisha's hypocrisy there was a Bible on the bedside cupboard.

Damn! Where the hell were they?

Gunfire sounded.

From the direction of the Ravens' shack!

* * *

"Cash should have returned by now," Berenice said, walking over to the Winchester. She picked it up. "I'm going to look for him."

"Is that wise, dear?" Gwendolyn said. "It's not as if we've heard any gunfire ..."

Unexpectedly, the door burst open and Elisha Price stood in the doorway, a .45 in his hand.

"You!" he exclaimed, eyes wide, his complexion paling, as if he'd seen a ghost.

Behind him stood Madeline, her face a mask of disbelief.

Hand shaking, Elisha raised the gun, aimed at Berenice.

Pluto the black cat jumped on his head, shrieking, claws out, scratching his face, and Elisha fired his revolver.

Berenice triggered the Winchester.

Wood splintered and Elisha yelled and then desperately flung off the cat and backed outside, his face streaked with blood, Madeline by his side.

Reloading, Berenice dashed to the door. She saw the pair running to her left, through the corral, amidst the horses. She looked over her shoulder and her heart skipped a beat.

Raven knelt by Gwendolyn who was sitting on the bed, her shoulder against the wall, a red patch on her arm. She said, "I'm all right. Go get them!"

Grabbing his Greener, Raven ran to Berenice's side and they both cautiously stepped out.

"Berenice!" Cash called. "Are you all right?" He sounded breathless, and then emerged from the shadows to her left.

"Where were you?" she demanded.

"More to the point, where are they?"

She pointed with the rifle barrel, further to their left. "They're desperate, Cash. I think they came to kill the Ravens."

"They can't hope to steal a horse," Raven said.

"Stay here," Cash ordered both of them. "This is my fight. I'm taking them in for trial."

Leaning against the wall, Berenice said, "Go ahead, be my guest. They're probably scared after seeing me. Thought I was a ghost."

"Well, they'll get a bigger shock when they see me!" he said and melted into the darkness.

* * *

Darkness wasn't absolute. The full moon provided enough light for Cash to see ahead of him several yards. He didn't particularly want to visit another graveyard so soon after emerging from the last one. At the best of times it could be an eerie place, but here now it seemed sepulchral, as if haunted. The Bells hotel would have been haunted, he felt sure, had it been left standing.

Having moved away from the light filtering from the shack's window and door, he could focus his eyes in the shadows now.

Silver moon-glow reflected off marble gravestones. Shadows from angels' wings created weird shapes like underworld creatures. He strained to hear any untoward sound, but he was wasting his time with the constant raucous noise of crickets.

Crouching behind a marble plinth that supported a huge cross, he scanned all around, seeking any movement in the gloom.

Then he spotted it, only a sliver of movement between two tombstones. Moving right to left.

Cautiously, moccasins not making the slightest sound, he darted to the left at an angle of interception.

The shape took form. It was a woman, her skirts lifted, running. Madeline. She was carrying a rifle in her right hand.

He chased after her, skipping over low-lying tombs, getting close, then she would swerve away, ducking down another row of memorials to the dead, as if they were in some bizarre dance.

Yet, gradually, he gained ground.

She suddenly stopped, turned, aimed and fired the rifle.

The explosion was loud, the nearby crickets ceased their noise, and the blast of light was blinding, for an instant recreating the moment in the hotel lounge.

But she'd missed.

Even as the after-glare cleared from his eyes, he dived headlong, his shoulder butting into her chest as she let off another shot.

They both fell to the ground.

Savagely, he wrestled the weapon from her, flung it into the night, and pinned her down with both hands.

"No, it can't be!" she yelled, eyes wide, staring, wriggling under him in vain.

"I'm no ghost," he said. "I'm flesh and blood."

"No, no, we buried you!"

"Wouldn't you like to think so? You're going to hang, damn you, you bitch!"

"Not if I can help it, Marshal!" snarled Elisha behind him.

Instinctively, Cash rolled over and in that same split-second Elisha fired.

Cash ignored the burning sensation as the bullet passed through the flesh at his side, and drew his Colt.

He fired three times.

Elisha Price fell against a marble angel, his arms snagged on the open wings. He hung there, blood oozing from two holes in his chest and one in his belly.

Keeping his gun aimed at Madeline, he strode over to the undertaker.

He wasn't quite dead, but he didn't have long before he'd be going to hell. His face was very badly scratched, an eyeball dangling on his bloody cheek.

"It hurts, I'm in pain," the undertaker murmured. "Please, for God's sake put me out of my misery!"

"Wouldn't you like to think so?"

"Yes ... Please, Marshal."

"No, I don't think so. For the sake of all those you've murdered, take your time and die slowly."

He turned to Madeline and knelt to examine her. The bullet that had passed through his side had penetrated her side also, but it wasn't fatal.

Tears filled her eyes.

He hoped the pain he felt was multiplied for her. "A noose waits for you, Mrs. Allan."

And Berenice stepped up and held the Winchester against Madeline's head, pulled the lever and chambered a round in the weapon.

TELL-TALE HEART

"Berenice, oh, Berenice!" Devon Penn paced his office, his features reflecting distress. "I only wish she had come to me sooner. You might have saved her brother!"

"You can't blame anyone but the felons, sir," Cash said. He rarely saw the chief agitated like this. He glanced across at Miles in the other chair, raised an eyebrow for moral support.

"Cash saved her life, sir," Miles offered. "And I prevented the wrong man being charged for murder. That has to be worth celebrating."

"I know, I know." Finally, Penn returned to the seat behind his desk. Irritably, he snatched a sheaf of papers from the tray on his right. "Thank God she didn't exact justifiable revenge on that awful Allan woman!"

Cash shrugged. "I wouldn't have blamed her, sir."

"And you wouldn't have arrested her, either, would you?"

"No. As you said, I would've regarded it as justifiable." They'd recovered Horace's money, and a lot more besides, from the luggage in the Annabel Lee Saloon. Berenice had deposited the money in the bank and had returned to Boston to resolve her brother's business affairs. When they'd parted on Cheyenne's station platform, she'd said, "I don't think I will see you again, Cash. I'm going to travel abroad, try to erase terrible memories—though not the time we spent together, I might add!"

"I won't forget you, either, Berenice."

And then the train took her out of his life.

"Well," Penn now said, "the woman spilled a few beans you weren't aware of, it seems. The three of them had a nice little thing going—waylaying the occasional rich guest, robbing them and disposing of their bodies. Her brother had heard about Horace Rohmer's business interest in the casino complex. He hired Corman who ambushed Horace on his way to the baron's spread. They took his money, then tied him up in the cellar and questioned him. Finally, he agreed to withdraw more money from the bank. After they got this second batch of money, they put him behind the wall of his room where he'd eventually succumb …"

"And the joss-sticks covered the smell?" Miles suggested.

"Yes." Penn shook his head. "The stink would have been overpowering until the bodies dried out. So far, they've found twenty-one corpses in the burned-out ruins of the hotel."

"Jesus!" Cash exclaimed.

"That's not all," Penn said. "Miles, I reckon you'll be interested to know that when a search was made of

Lenore Casino, they found something particularly gruesome."

"What was it, sir?" Cash asked, fascinated by Miles's parallel story.

Penn cleared his throat then said, "In a cupboard in the baron's office the sheriff found a glass case containing a human heart."

Miles groaned. "It has to be Lenore's."

"I don't doubt it," Penn said, "though that will never be proved."

"You could say," Cash added, "the baron was sick at heart."

†

ABOUT THE AUTHOR

Nik Morton has been writing for over 40 years and believes he's getting the hang of it now. Sold his first short story in 1971 and over 100 since, plus many articles, cartoons and illustrations. His first book sale didn't happen until 2007— quite a long wait, he reckons. Since then he's had 22 books published, with two more due out in 2016. His writing guide *Write a Western in 30 Days*, has reviewers recommending it for writers of all genres, not just westerns. He is busy writing the third book in 'The Tana Standish psychic spy' series, the fourth book in 'The Avenging Cat' series, and the third book in 'The Chronicles of Floreskand' series.

Write a Western in 30 Days—with plenty of bullet points!

"Morton has a brilliant way of condensing a great deal of information into manageable junks without sacrificing clarity or content. The resulting book works both as master class and as a refresher course."

"This is an excellent look at the writing process. It covers nearly everything and the advice contained here will apply to any genre."

A Fistful of Legends (Editor)
Sudden Vengeance
Spanish Eye
Blood of the Dragon Trees

- The Tana Standish psychic spy series
The Prague Papers (#1)
The Tehran Text (#2)

- The Avenging Cat series
Catalyst (#1)
Catacomb (#2)
Cataclysm (#3)

- Westerns writing as Ross Morton
The Magnificent Mendozas
The $300 Man
Old Guns
Blind Justice at Wedlock
Last Chance Saloon
Death at Bethesda Falls

- Fantasy writing as Morton Faulkner
Wings of the Overlord
To Be King

Gun smoke rises and blood spills . . .

In the town of Bear Pines, Mrs. Tolliver has announced she is running for the mayoral office. She's the first woman to run as a candidate which divides the residents and sets the town into a tailspin. U.S. Marshal Cash Laramie is sent in to maintain peace and order and to protect Tolliver and her family from powerful allies of the incumbent, Mayor Nolan. In a bid to force her to quit the race, things turn ugly ... and deadly. Surrounded by killers who will stop at nothing to make sure Mrs. Tolliver is not elected, Cash wires Cheyenne for assistance, but will help arrive in time?

www.beattoapulp.com